The 110 Lives

of

SJ Hudson

A Century & A Decade

GW00802001

By R.D. Bradley

ISBN-13: 9781089256373

For S&J, my greatest blessing

Nirvana

Do you know Nirvana? They say it's a state of supreme happiness that transcends the cycle of rebirth. Liberation from reincarnation. Well, it's not just a state of being... It's an actual place.

Fresh air breathed in like nectar. Decadent to inhale. Caressing to feel. And the brightest light, dizzyingly intense, softly burning up to illuminate endless expanses of unimaginable terrain; unbelievable workmanship. Dominated upon by something like a song; caught somewhere between the happiest jig and the most moving ballad.

Nirvana. Existence without flaw. Life, light, ecstasy. Perpetual bliss.

Ancient tradition founded in ageless regions talks of freedom of the soul. The highest aspiration of mankind. To be liberated from the cycle of re-birth.

A peasant; a prince; an emperor. A boy; a father; a daughter. An eagle; an ant.

Each time dying, and each time snapping awake the moment the heart stops beating to a different body, a new heartbeat, a new life.

Only to go over it again in still more varied forms:

A boatman; a priest; a layman. A juror; a geisha; a nun. A girl; a man... human; non-human – cycle after cycle, after cycle, until, finally, just... release.

Your eyes open. But this time the light doesn't hurt. This time there's no wailing in agony at beginning again. This time you've finally made it. Nirvana.

Though, what those souls still caught in the cycle of re-birth can never know is the secret that Nirvana holds. That hidden mystery of all of our much longed for and sought Nirvana. The secret that once you pass the stage of re-birth, once you conquer all cycles, Nirvana is not the end.

It's just a steppingstone – on which you can either climb up or stumble on...

The Keeper of Nirvana was tall and looming. Translucent and shimmering. Hair like tumbling wafts of snow, cascading, and in ceaseless motion like rushing waters framing her. Her eyes were twin jewels lit by orange flames. Her voice when she spoke; the sweetest lullaby... though her words stung deep like a thousand avenging wasps.

'It comes down to this,' she said. 'The ultimate qualifier. Does your soul have what it takes to attain Paradise? Existing, not in the world, but placed in a state of perpetual bliss – do you still remain virtuous, fulfilled and wholesome within such pleasure, or do you stumble, fall and return to the beginning?'

I stumbled.

Failing to maintain my humility and dignity in a perfect existence where everything was tailored to satisfy my every whim, too easily I forgot.

'You must leave here,' the Keeper continued, each word like the softest song but carrying the toughest blow.
'You must begin again.
GO.'
     The ground gave way.

I fell from Nirvana. My soul was swiftly demoted. Now I'm back where I started.
     I'm SJ Hudson and I have to relive a hundred and ten lives.

I

Chapter One

onsumate darkness lasted for a fraction of a second. I gasped awake. Eyes burning like they were set alight; snapping open, before almost immediately snapping shut again because the brightness was overwhelming. Not a soul-enhancing brightness of beauty like I'd known only moments ago, but a painful brightness that stung.

My head slammed between my ears; a throbbing ache made more excruciating by the glaring light. I gulped in desperate pockets of air. My skin prickled, alien and ill-fitting. Sounds I could not understand assailed my ears. It was as if I'd just come out of the womb. Raw and devastated.

But just when I was about to cry out in pain and confusion, wail like the new-born I actually was, I was struck. In a jolting flash and flood, memories cascaded into my mind. A wild rush instantaneously bringing me up to speed on the present life and my ultimate purpose.

Like a quieting wind, fragments of Nirvana breezed over me. My heart stopped racing. I took a deep breath. Slowly exhaled. And I opened my eyes again.

Groggily, shapes formed around me. Slowly, the body I was in began to take hold. I flexed my shoulders, cautiously raising myself off of the pillows I'd been lying on. And bringing a hand up to my still heavy head, I caught sight of it. A colourful tattoo right across my right hand palm. A spectacular and intricately formed design.

Curious, I would have taken a closer look at it, but the door opened, and a matronly woman came into my space – a large, crammed bedroom, I made out. She was small and plump with round, rosy cheeks.

'Oh, you're never still in bed at this time, are you?' she complained, bustling in. 'I would get on up and hurry on down to breakfast, if I were you.' She headed straight for the curtains, throwing them wide open. 'You know how impatient Smitty gets.'

My still hurting eyes shied away from the full brightness of the open windows for a moment, then adjusted. Lifting my head back up, I looked towards the open window. A stunning view lay exposed in front of me. Expansive grounds which we were at the very top of. Green and lush and damp with early autumn English rain.

A piercing pain suddenly stabbed at my chest looking out over the scene. Although I couldn't remember fully the landscapes of where I'd come from, in my heart of hearts I knew that this seemingly perfect country scene in front of me paled terribly in comparison to what I'd just lost.

Devastation once again washed over me.

'I have your uniform here,' the aproned housekeeper went on in cheerful tones, putting down the pile of neatly folded clothes she'd come in with. 'Freshly laundered and pressed.' She went about straightening the room, humming a chirpy tune.

In the grief sweeping over me I hardly noticed her at all now. I lay back against the pillows again, tearful and heartbroken. The weight of the loss of Nirvana so heavy upon me I thought I'd never have the strength to rise from the bed.

I didn't notice when the housekeeper's tune ended abruptly. Didn't even notice that she suddenly stood statue-still and straight in the middle of her bustling; unmoving as if frozen. But when she spoke, in an odd voice saying, 'Be conscious of your Atman.' I looked up sharply, jarred out of my misery.

'It is your real self beyond your ego,' she continued to say in that strange, unnatural voice.

I jumped up off the bed, covers and pillows flying everywhere. In a split second I was in front of her, grabbing her plump frame by the shoulders.

'Ezer? Ezer, is that you?' My heart was racing again. 'Thank God,' I breathed, beyond thrilled and happy to hear the Keeper of Nirvana's voice.

'Please, tell me. Tell me quickly, Ezer. What should I do? How do I go back to all my former lives? How do I relive them? Is it one in each season – or several? How do I go back? How do I do it?'

The housekeeper's eyes remained vacant, even in the face of my desperation. And, frustratingly, as if I hadn't spoken at all, Ezer only said, 'It is your spirit and your soul. It is the true self and essence which underlies existence.'

Impatiently, I shouted in the housekeeper's face, 'I know that Ezer. I know all about my Atman; my inner self and essence! But how do I go back? That's the real issue. How do I relive...?'

'It is worth fighting for,' she interrupted. 'Go forth in courage and boldness.'

'But Ezer... Ezer!'

The housekeeper's head slumped forward a moment, then quickly back up. She blinked a little, disoriented.

'Is everything alright now, Master Hudson?' It was her normal voice. Her normal self again.

I breathed a sigh of defeat. Ezer was gone.

'It's okay, Mrs Jenkins,' I said drawing away. 'Everything is okay.'

I didn't believe a word of that, of course. I was here, smack in the middle of a new life, and not sure about anything.

Mrs Jenkins took me at my word though, carrying on about her business, reminding me again how my grandfather wouldn't take kindly to my tardiness that morning.

And with nothing else for it, I was forced to shower and get dressed in record time before sprinting down the stairs towards the breakfast room.

Still not making it in time, however, and meeting up with Grandpa Smitty in the main hallway. He was fitted out in his usual gear of beige breeches, wellies and raincoat, already on his way out.

'Ah! Nice of you to finally show yourself, SJ,' he boomed gruffly. 'Not like you to get lost under the covers so long.' He was grabbing a wide brimmed hat from the cloak hanger. 'You're not sick, are you boy?'

'No gramps, I'm not sick,' I said, still trying to get a comfortable fit on my hastily pulled on school blazer.

'Good. Good. The car's waiting up front to take you to school. There's some paddocking on the Estate that needs looking to – I'm on my way there. Got to keep things running, ehy. Keep the old money-maker well-oiled, as they say. Or there'll be nothing for you or your father to inherit when I'm so many feet under.' He laughed heartily, turning on his heels to leave. But then stopped. 'Oh, which reminds me. Skype that lackadaisical father of yours and, his accomplice in tardiness, your mother! They complain they haven't spoken to you in eons.'

Eons? I hardly thought. What did either of them know about eons? They had no memories of the past like I did. A *past* past – of life lived before; of Nirvana won and heartbreakingly lost.

No. My parents definitely had no idea about eons.

But I would dutifully Skype the artist-heir to Carbarney Manor and the dutiful muse who'd accompanied him on a painting trip around Europe for the better part of a year.

I would Skype and chat like everything was normal, like everything was fine and I wasn't haunted each moment by half-remembered visions of perfect Nirvana. This, apparently, was my life now.

How would Skyping and playing along to the constraints of this life help me get back to Nirvana? How would it save my soul?

Watching my grandfather stride purposefully out the door, I had no idea.

Half turning away, my eye caught my reflection in an ornate heirloom-type full-length mirror across the hall. I took it in again. This new physical form I had.

Average height, average weight. An unruly curly top of jet-black hair. Caramel skin and soft brown eyes. And, fully in uniform, I was every bit the sixteen-year-old schoolboy.

'Had a good look, have you?' Mrs Jenkins teased, appearing behind me with a feather duster and dustpan. 'You still the best lookin' lad in the South – take heart!' She laughed, bustling off as quickly as she'd come.

I reached for my school bag in the cloak cabinet. As I did so my eyes once more fell on the tattoo blazoned across my right palm.

It was shaped like an amulet, the design intricate and winding; solid golds, greens and bleeding reds interwoven together to form the pattern. A spidery outline of what could have been the figure of a man laid out like a map.

Studying it closely, it was an effort to force myself to stop. Eventually, I scrunched up my fists, scrunching the drawings too.

I had to do this. I had to live this life and somehow find the way back to where I truly belonged.

Heart still heavy, but hardened now with determination, I picked up my satchel and marched to the door.

Chapter Two

I had a best friend, apparently. Patrick Astley.

'Oi!' Patrick gave a smile and a small salute as I stepped out of one of my grandfather's cars in front of the school.

In this life, we'd been mates since we were little kids, growing up together in the town of Carbarney just as our fathers had done – even now attending the same secondary school as they'd done. Carbarney College.

From many long conversations, I'd got that the school had in a way failed to accommodate my artist father's so-called "free spirit" and he'd hated every minute of it. But in direct converse, the opposite had been true of Patrick's dad. He'd gone on to excel. He was a respected MP now, with every expectation that Patrick would not only follow in his footsteps but that he would totally one up his father by being no less than Prime Minister at the end of it all.

I thanked the driver and returned Patrick's wave. We met up just outside of the grand hall where a congestion of other pupils were already beginning to line up for morning assembly.

'You still scrounging rides?' Patrick laughed. 'What happened to the driver's licence?'

'Just turned sixteen last month, mate. Give us time!' I countered gruffly. He always did forget there were almost two years between us. And he ignored my tone, no doubt too excited to care much about anything except the prospect of his full hopes being realised that morning.

First assembly of the new school year. The new prefect body was coming in, including the new Head Prefect, and it would all be announced at this assembly. And Patrick, being Patrick, obviously took it as standard that he would be bagging not only Prefect but also Head Prefect.

For me, it was frustrating trivia that was forced on me when all I really wanted was to get on with knowing how in heck, in this seemingly petty and uninspiring new life, I was going to find my ascent to Nirvana.

Nirvana. Nirvana. Nirvana.

It was consuming me.

But for my "bestie" Patrick, with his perfectly combed down brown hair; his pristine merit badges decorated uniform; his arrogant, stiff posture, and his pale, pinched face, this particular moment meant more than life itself.

The Head Prefect of Carbarney College almost always ended up further along the line as Prime Minister of the country. It was almost a tradition.

And just as his father expected it, Patrick expected it for himself also. As much as his father saw him in a grand light, Patrick saw himself in an even grander light. His own expectations for himself exceeded even those of his father.

And towards the close of assembly when the new prefects were named and called up on stage to receive their badges, Patrick was the most smug, most haughty of the bunch, standing in the line-up on stage more than ready to receive the title that would be the threshold to his greatness.

It no doubt came as a gut-wrenching shock to him when the school Master read out his name with the word "Deputy" attached to it.

Patrick Astley, Deputy Head Prefect.

They had to call him twice, he was so dazed. Finally, he hesitantly stepped forward to accept the badge.

Then when the Master announced the Head Prefect and it was a girl, I could almost feel the rage emanating from him, even from where I was sitting at the back of the hall in the juniors' section. I sighed. Not only had he been side-lined. It had to have been by a girl, and it had to have been *her*.

Thato Singh smiled brightly as she stepped forward. Bright white teeth set in a dark-chocolate brown face. Tall, with an athletic built and a head full of long, light coloured braids, she was a very pretty girl. Most of the boys in the school fancied Thato, but never Patrick. Threatened by her brilliance academically and by her equal capabilities in sport, he'd always hated her.

And judging from the eyeballs of fire he was throwing her way as she shook hands with the Master and accepted her badge, he would be loathing her more now.

The first thing to come out of his mouth when assembly ended and all students filed to lessons was a hot, '*Can you believe it!*' almost jumping me in the corridor.

'Yeah, mate, that sucks for you.' I tried to inflect empathy in my voice and failed. I was just so distracted and weighed on by other thoughts, wanting nothing more than to go my way and figure things out. But again, Patrick hardly noticed. He was fuming.

He let out a tirade of venom against the supposed malicious, ungrateful school as well as on the demerits of Thato Singh and how, she of all people, least deserved the honour of Head Prefect.

When it looked like he wouldn't stop venting and raging, I cut in. 'You coming this way for your first lesson?'

Patrick shook his head, brows furrowed deep and his face more pinched that usual. 'Nah. I've got Hall Monitor duty already –

and with *her*, if you can believe it. How I'm going to bear this whole friggin' year, I don't even know.'

Then like a bad joke, the girl he'd just been tearing into appeared behind him.

'Hi Patrick,' she said, and I almost laughed to see the way Pat jumped.

'Oh, Thato!' he looked up at her in surprise. 'Hi!'

She smiled. Her hands were linked behind her back and she stood straight, her full height a head above Patrick, who veered on the short side.

'Isn't your friend running late for class?'

I perked up. 'Oh, yes. Yes. On my way!'

As I left them, Patrick gave me that *See-what-I-mean-she's-horrific* look. I could only shake my head and go on my way. To me, Thato was rather more intriguing than horrific. Raised in an Indian-British household but originally from unknown beginnings somewhere in the east of Africa, she wasn't like many people around Carbarney.

But as painful and dramatic as Patrick was making the whole saga between them seem, I definitely had bigger fish to fry. I sure as heck wasn't marooned in this dull life to be drawn into the middle of a feud between two high schoolers.

The Keeper still hadn't explained to me in full.

Exactly how was this quest back to Nirvana going to work? How could I make things right? How could I triumph and regain everything I'd lost? And how could I do all that when I barely knew which way was which?

It was a heady relief when halfway along the corridor I stumbled on a mop and turned around to see a janitor staring down at me with a blank expression on his face. When he spoke it was Ezer.

'Follow me,' she said briefly, before quickly walking away.

Faint with relief, I followed. She stopped behind a large pillar overlooking the expanse of the school grounds in the now deserted quad area. I joined her there.

'Ezer,' I breathed, 'It's so good to have you here again. I've been so desperate...'

'Just listen, and listen well,' she was firm. 'I have to remind you once again of the Dharma Shastra – those three stages to soul freedom. Of course, *Virtue* is the first one you must attain. Then there is *Artha*; material possession or wealth. And, lastly, *Kama* – that emotional fulfilment every soul desires for itself.

Only when you have mastered these three will there be *Moksha*; freedom of your soul forever. Only then will you be able to return to Nirvana.

And, as you now know, from Nirvana it is on to Paradise.

But first the three Dharma Shastra must be fulfilled.'

'How Ezer?' I begged again, ever more desperately. 'How will I travel to my former lives when I'm stuck here, *now* – in Carbarney; in this life?'

One of the janitor's large, calloused hands reached out to envelop one of mine.

'The Amulet of Atman. I have carved it upon the palm of your right hand for this very purpose.'

I opened the hand that the amulet was drawn on in vivid, bold ink, as she continued to speak;

'Every night you will close your eyes to sleep, my *ladaka*,' the endearing Hindi term for "little one" was heartfelt and kind, 'and every night you will travel back to who you once were. You will not sleep but you will live... again. One night. One life. One year.'

'A year?' I looked up, jarred. 'I'll be living a full year of each life!'

The Keeper sensed my dismay and sense of burden at the prospect. Lightly, the hand that had held mine rose up to my shoulder. She squeezed gently.

'Let this not weigh hard on you, *Ladaka*. A year can come in many parts, and a life can be comprised of just the fragments of that year – days, weeks, hours, minutes. A year is only the maximum.'

'How will I get back?'

The Keeper smiled. 'When the task you need to complete to attain one of the Dharma Shastra is complete then return is a matter of course. But make note, my *ladaka*, if you do not pass the test then it will be on to another life, on to another night. Life after life – night after night, until you do. Thought there is a limit, *Ladaka*. For Nirvana's sake remember that. One hundred and ten lives. That is all you get. All three Shastra of the Dharma must be attained before the expiry of the one hundred and ten lives. Failing that, my *ladaka,* I am afraid you will be forfeit – entirely.'

I did not blink away from her stern look or shrink from the magnitude of the trial she'd just set before me. I was being ripped apart by desperation for Nirvana. My pain and hunger would be my determination. I was confident of success – immediate success. With the resolve I felt, I wouldn't even need that many lives to fulfil the Dharma Shastra.

'You are strong, my *ladaka*,' the Keeper affirmed. 'I have no doubt in your abilities. Only stay the course and never lose faith. Many are the distractions and pitfalls that will arise. But believe me when I say it is all to build you up.'

'And this hacking in my chest?' I looked at her with eyes blurred with tears. 'This ferocious pain in my heart. Will it ever go away?' A tear ran down my cheek.

Ezer's eyes burned back at me, full of compassion. She shook her head. 'My *ladaka*, I know it is hard, but the pain you feel at this moment is nothing compared to what you would feel if I had not taken away most of your memories of Nirvana. It was a kindness, *Ladaka*. And the hazy images and feelings you have of it now are only rudimentary. Just enough to keep you going forwards in your journey. If you were to lose all the memory, then you would lose Nirvana. You would be lost to it and not even know it.'

'Oi! SJ! Is that you, mate?' It was Patrick, calling from a few feet away. With one final smile and glint of an eye, Ezer was gone and the janitor came back to himself. He fumbled for a bit, gruffly cursing before going on his way.

Patrick trotted over to me. 'Mate, you shouldn't be out here at this time. Lessons began ages ago. If that She-Wolf Thato catches you it'll be detention for a month! You better get, mate.'

'Yeah. I'm going. I'm going.'

'Catch you later – after school?' Patrick called after me as I walked on.

I raised a salute. 'Yeah mate. Later.'

I clock-watched the day away, counting every minute and second until nighttime came, promising release from the petty constraints I found myself in and I could actually truly live again.

I was impatient when finally darkness fell, the Manor growing absolutely still and quiet, giving the much longed for chance to retire to my rooms for the night. With only one last obligation, as I'd promised Grandpa Smitty. I had to Skype call the people who were my parents here.

I sat at my desk, the lamp beside shining a soft glow. The laptop screen lit up almost immediately with Vicky and Tommy Hudson anticipating the call and quickly picking up just a second after I'd dialled.

Mum smiled. 'Hey darling!'

Dad waved. 'Finally, son. We thought you'd never ring.'

'Hi mum. Hi dad.' I obliged. 'How is...' I struggled to piece together where they should be now in their Euro trip.

'Malta, honey,' Mum supplied. 'We're in Malta.' She pushed back her heavy, dark dreadlocks, soft brown eyes shining, looking every bit the untroubled bohemian with her colourful dress and rattling jewellery. Her skin was a deeper shade of brown from undoubted hours in the Mediterranean sun. A sharp contrast to Dad who never could take too much sun and seemed rather raw red in the face now with sunburn.

It made me smile a little how physically polar opposites they were yet how similar their spirits. "Flighty, fairy" types, Grandpa Smitty liked to term them gruffly. Tommy ever searching for inspiration – according to Grandpa – while a fence-sitting Vicky, half free spirit, half responsible realist, tended to be pulled along into his drifter ways.

For me, though, they were just two souls living their truth, making their way towards their own Nirvana. I listened to them as dutifully as any son, mind partly attentive, focused mostly on thoughts of my own Nirvana. It was a relief when the artists' ever demanding duties called to them away once more and the call wrapped up.

I would have happily jumped straight to bed, but there was a knock on the door before Grandpa Smitty came in.

'So, how was the first day back at school?' He advanced further into the room, himself already in pyjamas and night robe.

'Not bad,' was all I could thing to say. Not: I'd barely registered any of my surroundings or anything else going on because all I'd been thinking about since talking to Ezer was falling asleep and having my first do-over.

'And did you Skype your parents?'

I gave a nod as he took a seat beside me on the bed.

'Did they have much to say for themselves? Oh, no, don't answer that. I know they did. Great talkers Vicky and Tommy, of course. These free types always are.' He scoffed. 'Ah, those two. Your father quitting law school to become a painter, and now your mother and this "hiatus" from her firm to follow him around Europe as he does his nonsense. Ag, but it's their virtue, I suppose.'

I looked up at the word. Virtue. I was suddenly alert, thinking it might be Ezer again. My spine stiffened, but relaxed again when Grandpa Smitty gave a gruff laugh and went on, his ordinary self;

'Lands, titles – trust me, they count for little when it comes to the make-up of a man's virtue. I can't say that I like your parents' choices or their lifestyles very much, but I suppose there's something to be said for following the heart – gut instinct, you know.'

Musingly, he got up, patting me on the shoulder fondly.

'Get some sleep, boy.'

Oh, I wholly intended to Papa, I thought, using the term I'd grown into the habit of calling him from childhood; him being a more present a figure than my constantly travelling dad had been.

He closed the door behind him, and I let out a breath of relief.

Frustratingly, though, my phone beeped. I looked at the screen to see Patrick's ID. He was texting me about football – some long-winded rubbish about leagues and scores. Then about Thato Singh; full-on moaning about being passed over for Head Prefect.

I shook my head, quickly texting back;

Dude, you're obsessed. Get some sleep!

Then I switched off the phone completely. I really didn't have the time of day for Patrick or his Thato. I had lives to live.

Releasing a long breath, I lay back on the bed. As I closed my eyes, the amulet on my palm warmed and my skin throbbed gently. Then a burst of a burn.

I didn't fall asleep. I lived again.

Different time and place.

Different body and life.

Normandy, France
1120

My eyes flashed open, almost as instantly as they'd shut. In a split second I was staring up at a new moon in a cloudless sky, my heart immediately thumping hard in my chest. The iciness of the wind, blowing bitingly, hit me square in the face. The sound of crashing waves, laughter, music and merry chatter; all loud with a force I hadn't expected.

And suddenly there was rocking beneath my feet. I half toppled over with the unexpected unsteadiness of the ground under me. But in the next moment realisation came that it wasn't "ground" at all. It was hard, varnished wood.

Luckily, I managed to find my footing in time and only lost the jewelled goblet I'd been clinging to. Dark wine spilled over into the sea along with the goblet. I steadied myself with a hand tightly gripping the side of the ship.

My little mishap attracted a rush of giggles from a group of girls I now noticed surrounding me. They were all pretty girls, dressed in medieval-style flowing rich gowns of detailed design and with hair done up in formal, beaded and jewelled styles.

This made me look down at my own clothes. Silken garments stitched with gold thread, gleaming richly – and not just general richness; the absolutely *royal* rich kind.

The wind picked up in that moment and the ship rocked again. Something almost slipped from my head. In a quick movement I managed to save the slip, my hand coming into contact with cold round metal. A crown.

'William! William!' The yells of a girl striding towards me cut through my thoughts. She was dressed as ornately as everyone else but unlike the other girls she had a brightly jewelled tiara on her head. She was in her teens, same as I was. And I realised that I knew her. Knew her very well, in fact.

'Matilda,' I said softly, recognising her as my half-sister.

But just as I stepped up to meet her with a smile, she grabbed my arm in a furious grip, and shook it.

'Stephen's leaving,' she said angrily.

Catching my blank expression, she rolled her eyes, throwing my arm back at me. 'Remember him? Your cousin! Far more sensible that you'll ever be! He says he's got a stomach upset or something, but I know for a fact all that's really wrong with him is that he's sick to death of all this *nonsense*.' She had a small hand to the hip now. 'How much more partying are you planning? Aren't you ever fed up of being this non-stop carousing idiot? Really, you have no dignity, William. No virtue...'

As she yelled the last word in my face the floodgates of my mind opened. My whole life here came tumbling into my brain in less than a second.

William the Atheling. That's who I was. Son of Henry the first of England. Grandson of William the Conqueror. I was heir to the English and Norman thrones.

And – it hit me hard like a punch to the stomach – I also happened to be one of the most spoiled and arrogant youths to ever walk the planet.

Here I was now, in true Atheling style – on board the royal White Ship, celebrating myself and my charmed life: At only seventeen years old, with a new royal wife, new rich lands gifted to me on a platter, and recently titled *rex designates*; the King Designate, co-King with my father. Celebrating all this glory with the richest and most titled teens of the Anglo-Norman elite. Conceit beyond belief. Zero virtue.

I looked round at the partying going on around me again. Spoiled, unimaginably wealthy kids exactly like me. Laughing, drinking, dancing, numbing their young lives away with excess. We were supposed to have left port hours ago on the way back to England, following after my father, the King, but we'd delayed ourselves with the unending celebrations.

I caught sight of the light of the moon glinting atop the waves our ship sat on. The wind was gathering strength and roughly rocking both. In total panic I looked at my angry sister who'd just been going on about Stephen leaving the ship. The hammering in my chest began again in full force.

She was right. Matilda was so right. We had to stop. We had to stop immediately.

It was past midnight and tonight was *the* night. I remembered it well. But I was determined, things wouldn't happen as they'd done before. Tonight I would live; live *and* bag virtue – number one of my Dharma Shastra.

Gone was going to be the pompous arse I'd grown up to be. This was it – to right all the wrongs of the past; change the course of history. William the Atheling would not die in the shipwreck of the White Ship. I would live to be the king I never got to be first time round.

'You're right,' I said to Matilda, who nearly toppled over herself with shock and disbelief. In all the years, from childhood onwards, she'd never heard those words come out of my mouth; ever.

'What?' she could only stare at me.

I nodded emphatically. 'You're right. We have to get off this ship. We have to –'

My words were cut off as the boat rocked forwards. Another girl came up behind Matilda.

'Too late,' she announced cheerfully. 'The Captain's already set off. He can barely stand, he's so drunk, but he professes he can get us to England before your father.' Her sparkling eyes were laughing into my own.

In that moment I knew her too. But not as I'd known Matilda, recognising her as a part of this life. This girl just wasn't Matilda's best friend who we'd all grown up together with, this girl was something more. In the infinity of time, before this, after this, I knew her and recognised her soul.

It dawned on me suddenly. In many lives; present, past and future, she was and always would be there.

Her soul – it was Patrick's Thato Singh. Only that she wasn't Patrick's at all. She was... mine.

In the thralls of my realisations, I made a move towards her. But I was knocked full off my feet in the next instance. We hadn't been away from shore two minutes before the ship crashed.

A sharp, rocky outcrop punched that infamous, fatal hole in the wooden prow of the White Ship.

At the impact, the entire ship shook. So forcefully that many of the passengers, my young friends and relatives, who I'd been celebrating life with just moments before, were hurled into the water by the violence of the crash.

Petrified screams and struggle followed. The fine robes that many of us had been wearing turned to death nooses. Soaked with freezing ocean water, they quickly became unmanageable, heavy death traps that made it impossible to even try to swim. The cries of drowning were agony in the chill night air.

On the wooden floor in the vessel, I drew myself up, scrambling to my feet, shaking off what I could of the freezing sea water rapidly pouring in. Helping Matilda up also, I scanned round desperately for Thato – Angelique du Bois as she was in this life. Clambering after her as soon as I caught sight of her crouched to the side of the starboard.

Some of the crew were trying hopelessly to bail out the torrents rushing the ship, and I had to fight my way through the desperate pandemonium to get to Angelique.

I had almost made it when I was grabbed by others of the crew. They kept talking about a lifeboat they'd thrown over the side of the sinking ship for me. They weren't interested in my protest as I tried to tell them I had to get someone first. And they wouldn't let me take a step further – actually grabbing me, dragging me forcefully towards the lifeboat.

I was the most important cargo onboard and they would manhandle me with brute force, as necessary, to safety.

I was thrown, fighting into the lifeboat, and restrained firmly with multiple pairs of hands. As they began to row me away from the carnage, I heard more splashes as still more people fell overboard, and I didn't have to imagine it to be Matilda or Angelique because as both cried out to be saved, their anguished voices rang in my ears until they were all I could hear.

We were rowing further and further away, the safety of Barfleur harbour on the horizon. I shook off the hands restraining me. Tears poured over my face.

'I am your Prince!' I cried to the men. 'I am your Prince and you will do as I say!'

Among many others, the shouts and cries of my half-sister and Angelique continued on more desperate still. And theirs were the only ones I heard.

This was it. The very moment of destiny. We could paddle away to safety and I would live to be the glorious king I now knew I had it in me to be. Or we could turn back for Matilda and Angelique; risking certain death... Just like the first time.

I saw Grandpa Smitty's face then, on the surface of those choppy waves. I could hear his voice as it'd been right before I'd closed my eyes. Clearly, his words on virtue came back to me.

Virtue didn't have to be about lands and titles, didn't it? Maybe not even about becoming a great king. To follow the heart... instinct. That was what mattered most.

I saw Thato in my mind's eye. All the forms and faces I remembered of her. All the forms and faces I'd cared for deeply through our many lives together.

Without a moment's more hesitation, I ordered the men to go back for them.

In minutes, we'd fished the two spluttering girls out of the icy ocean water. They were shivering and shaken. I held Angelique tightly in my arms, wonderfully familiar feelings washing over me like the waves around us.

But it took only seconds for our small skiff to be rushed on by the other desperate drowning people.

I looked into Angelique's eyes, eyes that were the windows to a soul I was connected to through space and time. They were the last thing I saw before the skiff was capsized and sunk.

The rushing ocean waves engulfed us both.

Chapter Three

I woke up gasping and spluttering in bed. Dismay setting in that I was no closer to virtue than when I'd first closed my eyes.

At Carbarney College that day it was with different eyes that I looked at Thato Singh.

I watched her closely throughout. At assembly; in the corridors; as she made her way to her classes. Discombobulated and torn, I basically remember it all. Our entire history together across centuries. And it made me more than a little desperate to connect with her again in this life. It almost consumed me as much as the yearning for Nirvana.

At break, I couldn't help but watch her closer. Lost in my own year group of boisterous boys, I looked over to where she sat, over and over again during the half hour we all had outside after lunch.

Memories rushed my mind, until all I could think of was how in the world would I bridge the gap that existed between us now?

I was over here with the Year 11s, she was over there with the sixth formers. How would I ever connect with her when we were basically in different stratosphere here. Head Prefect and basic pupil.

I had multiple lives lined up, multiple lives to prepare for, yet now, all that seemed to occupy me was this one soul; this girl.

I mean, she'd been my anchor over centuries, and as the situation was for at the moment, I desperately needed an anchor – just one thing to ground me in all the total craziness I faced.

But watching her laughing away easily with her friends, and getting up to leave with them, straightening a blazer whose front was almost completely covered with honour badges, I was left a little crestfallen. She didn't even register me.

'So, it didn't work out.' The janitor was suddenly beside me raking up leaves.

The statement was plainly matter of fact.

I shot a quick look to the guys sitting near me in the gazebo. They were full occupied exchanging funny memes off of each other's phones, and barely noticed the janitor. I sighed, running a hand through my hair.

'Not quite,' I replied. 'Anyway, I thought you said a year – that it was a year I got each time to fix things? Last night was more like five minutes, and the next thing I knew I was shipwrecked and plunging to my death!'

Ezer smiled. 'Yet here you are. And what I said was *up to* a year. There's a difference.'

I rolled my eyes, wrapping my blazer tighter around me against a chill breeze that reminded me of my Normandy misadventure.

Ezer looked me squarely in the eyes,

'You failed, *Ladaka.*'

My shoulders slumped as she went on,

'You made the same mistake again – choosing the personal over the greater good.'

I flared up at that. 'Greater good? You have to be joking, right! What greater good was there in leaving – saving myself while everyone I cared about drowned... while *she* drowned? How could I have pushed off and left her to drown?'

Ezer briefly put a calming hand to my shoulder, and she was completely earnest. 'My *ladaka*, Angelique's journey was over as soon as she hit the water. But because you went back for her – because of your choice that night King Henry died without a male heir, which caused your cousin Stephen Blois to step in and challenge your sister for the throne. You, and everybody else, know that that led to the bloodiest civil war this country has ever known. Many peopled suffered; thousands upon thousands died.

There can be no virtue in leading to the deaths of so many people. Try again, *Ladaka*. Don't make the same mistakes.'

She left.

The janitor continued to rake away, now humming a low tune, oblivious to me.

'Hey, you loitering again?'

It was Patrick, smiling broadly. I blinked. I hadn't realised that everyone else was streaming away from the fields back to the main buildings.

'Better get stepping; the She-Wolf will be prowling soon, and you don't want to get caught in her fangs.' He laughed at his own joke.

I walked with him a little reluctantly. I knew he was talking about Thato. And, to be honest, I would have liked nothing more than to carry on sitting out there and be found out by her; even just for a telling off.

'You coming tonight, yeah?' Patrick was saying. 'The arcade. On my team, as always, yeah?'

I nodded, distractedly. Every now and again guys from the College formed teams and competed against each other at the local arcade. I was always with Patrick.

I would keep tradition and go, even though arcade games were my least focus right now.

A Friday night, the go-to mega arcade of Carbarney was packed. Clusters of local kids happy to be done with the first week back at school grouping together, animatedly talking, laughing and getting into the full gaming spirit.

I found my own cluster, a group of guys made up mostly of Patrick's form. One or two of the guys I knew from my own class, but we weren't particularly friendly. It was a gaming league Patrick headed up and we usually divided into smaller teams and tallied scores against each other.

That night Patrick had me on his team – as per usual – but I was half-hearted about it; distracted. It was an actual relief, as the competing began, when I saw some girls from school walk in; Thato now out of uniform and decorated blazer, tall and looking chic in a bright yellow skirt worn with a wispy dark blouse. Her coppery coloured braids hung low over her shoulders. I took in a breath, duty to my teammates immediately taking a far back seat.

I felt like my moment had come. I didn't have the words exactly – didn't even know what my plan was actually, but I knew I had to talk to her.

And exactly because I didn't really have a plan and didn't know what to say, it got to the point where I was almost semi-stalking!

Dropping my band of gamers without pause, I gravitated towards her; ever watching without knowing what I was watching for.

My subtlety was about as good as my patience. Non-existent. She caught me out pretty quickly.

Designated to get drinks for her own friends, she stopped by the juice machine, making a sharp turn, coming to face me full on with sparkling dark eyes.

'Are you following me?'

The words were blunt, and I was gobsmacked.

A cheeky smile payed on her lips. 'You're a bit obvious, don't you think?'

With an awkward laugh, I exhaled, not bothering to deny it.

'You're Viscount Patrick's BFF, aren't you?' she said snootily.

'Well, pretty sure he's just a Baron for now – viscount, no.' I replied in the same cheeky tone. 'And, yes, we are close.'

'Ah, just Baron Patrick then – less pretentious!' She rolled her eyes humorously. 'Well, I hope that arse-lord is not too close behind you right now though.' It was a joke, but she quickly backtracked, 'Sorry, shouldn't call him an arse. You're his mate after all.'

'No need to say sorry. We know people for what they are, doesn't mean we are less their friend or care for them any less.'

The jokiness went out of Thato a little. She blinked. 'Wow. Where did that come from. So mature. Aren't you like twelve?' A streak of mischievousness luminated her eyes again.

I laughed. 'Sixteen, actually. I'm sixteen.'

Thato shrugged. 'Same thing!'

Again, I laughed, surprised by this side of her. At school she was always so serious and no non-sense dutiful. But here she was playful and light-hearted. More of the spirit I'd fallen for decade after decade in times past.

I offered to help with the drinks for her friends. Instantly easy with one another we did it together, and when the drinks were dutifully served and finished and Thato excused herself from the group, I went with her.

'You sure you want to tag along?' she asked. 'Trust me, it's not very exciting at my aunt's shop. It's a small textile shop. Indian fabrics bursting at every point, and I literally just need to drop materials for her. A twenty-minute thing.'

'It's fine.' I said. 'I'll keep you company along the way, and I will.' I affirmed. 'And *Lord* Patrick's not going to be in a huff coz I stole you away from the team?'

We were almost at the door. 'You said it'll be quick, and my turn's not even come up yet. He's cool.'

The night air was very fresh when we stepped outside, the streets Carbarney town centre quiet as most shops were boarded up for the night. Making the short walk to Thato's aunt's shop, there was an easy, natural companionable connection between us. I was sure she couldn't help but feel it too. And I wished I could get the words to tell her – to fully describe in detail the extent of the connection between us.

Instinctively, I knew that it went against nature and the laws of the schism that governed the world, and I knew for sure Ezer wouldn't approve. Yet I so badly wanted to tell Thato. Just unburden my soul and show her how there was more – much, *much* more – to existence; what spiritual, transcendent beings we all were, connected in ways she couldn't even imagine. I wanted to remind her of what we'd always been to each other.

Before I could harness the courage or form the words, we arrived at her aunt's shop.

It was a small boutique store, and although fully lit up inside, a closed sign hung over the door.

Thato dug out a key from her purse, and once she'd unlocked the door, we stepped inside. It was like being engulfed in a sea of fine, brightly coloured fabrics.

The lady at the till immediately looked up.

A frown darkened her face. 'What took you so long?' she complained in an exasperated voice to Thato. 'I told you I needed that lace soon as you picked it up from home.'

'Sorry,' Thato only said, sheepishly fishing in her purse once again to get out the needed lace. She added that she'd stopped off at the arcade for drinks and popcorn with friends.

The woman left the till to grab the lace from Thato's hands. She was a short portly Indian woman with long dark hair and dressed fully in traditional robes, complete with henna tattoos and bejewelled forehead.

'And who's this?' she asked, directing a disinterested gaze at me.

'Oh! He's a friend from school.' Thato replied. 'His name's SJ.'

But the aunt had lost interest already, shuffling to a different end of the room expressing worries about not having enough time and about how a bride was coming in for a fitting tomorrow and not being sure if the garments would be ready on time.

Then that was quickly followed up by complaints of how overwhelmed she was; how little help she had from those around her.

Thato looked at me. I looked at her. She raised her shoulders with a helpless smile. I could tell she was eager to retreat from the tirade.

When her aunt finally paused for breath, Thato jumped in with;

'Okay, Aunt Nadra! So, we'll just get going now...' But before she could even begin to say the word bye, Aunt Nadra spun round.

'No. Go? Now, when I'm so overwhelmed!' she was incredulous. 'I have a bridal fitting in the morning; I need to finish off the dress – tonight. And there's new fabrics that still need to be sorted in the backroom before the store opens. No excuses Thato; into the storeroom, please. I can't do everything myself!' Without pause for response she immediately set about her own agenda, gathering different fabrics.

Thato gave me an apologetic smile. 'So, I won't be heading back to the arcade any time soon.'

'Hm, I don't know about that,' I replied. 'Two pairs of hands are better than one.'

'No, really?' Thato was genuinely surprised. 'Come on. No, SJ, I don't expect you to while away half your Friday night sorting fabrics! It's okay; get back to the arcade; finish your competitions. This is basically my life right now – I always handle it; I am a master fabric sorter.'

'And I have a varied skill set that would surprise you. And having to listen to Patrick screaming at everybody with his competitiveness – please, I can do without that for one Friday night!'

Thato smiled all that brighter. 'Erm, okay, let's go sort some fabric then. I am warning you though it's a crazy amount of fabric.'

And she wasn't joking. The storeroom was packed tight with boxes and piles of loose colourful fabric lying everywhere. It would definitely take a while. Neither of us wanting to be there all night we stuck right into it.

'So,' Thato said when the initial light-hearted joking and laughter between us toned down as we folded and sorted. 'You must be mind-boggled by my family situation.'

I tossed yet one more rainbow fabric into a corner pile. 'I wouldn't say mind-boggled, but it's interesting.'

'Yeah, well, the long and short of it is that I was adopted. Not by Aunt Nadra and Uncle Ishaan. Uncle Ishaan is my dad's cousin – my adopted dad, but just my dad, coz he's the only dad I've ever known. Him and my mum adopted me when I was a baby. But then mum got sick.' She stopped folding and took a breath. 'She died.'

Close enough to lean over, I put a hand over hers. She understood the gesture and gave a teary smile.

'I know. It was... hard. I mean, she was the best mum. Like tender, loving, good... just everything a wonderful mum should be. My dad told me that that had always been her dream, ever since he'd known her; to be a mum. And she was so devoted to that; so devoted to me. She always said that I was the crowning glory of her life.' Tears were streaming down her face now. 'After all the years she'd tried and failed to get pregnant, then I came along. This little baby from an east African village somewhere. She saw a picture of me through an agency and she just knew. Just knew that I was hers. And we became a family, you know. And we were so happy. Oh gosh SJ, I wish you could have known us in those days. It really was just perfect.

But it wouldn't last long. I was only eleven when the cancer came, and it was so quick and aggressive that by the time I was twelve she was gone.'

I hugged her tight. Her pain felt like my own pain. How many times had she held me like this through the decades? Too many to count, I remembered.

'And your dad?' I asked gently. 'Where is he now?'

She let out a breath. 'Well... Dad. Yeah, dad. He's just something else. Apparently, after mum died, he had some kind of "spiritual awakening". He'd always been really into Veda – you know, like the Hindu bible. Actually, what he liked to refer to himself as was; "an avid student of Veda". And he liked to say that he was "twice born" – whatever that means.'

My heart stopped.

Twice born?

Her father recognised himself as a *Twice Born*. It was one of the highest statuses of the reincarnated soul. The initiation was receiving a sacred thread as a boy, marking your spirit's high status.

'So, anyway,' Thato went on, 'after mum passed, he said it was his sacred duty to fulfil the four stages of a Twice Born. Yeah, I know. Bit nuts. So, what does he do? He "retires from life" – stage three, apparently – becoming a hermit.

I mean, it was fine for a while. He'd done quite well in his surgical practice over the years, so there were savings and stuff. But then came stage four... Renunciation...'

I knew *Renunciation* very well. I had almost been there in a few lives back. It was called Samnyasa. A person gave up the world totally. Took only one robe, a bowl and a staff that was it. In order to develop devotion. They give up... everything.

'Your father is Samnyasa,' I said matter-of-factly.

Thato nodded. 'Emptied his back accounts. Gave all the money away. Gave away the house, cars, clothes... everything. Last I heard of him he was in India somewhere, chasing Moksha.'

Wow, I thought to myself. The Moksha. The final step before Nirvana. Her father was just like me. Only that he'd fulfilled everything he needed to fulfil in a single life – not like me and the century and a decade it would take; and also, not like me he hadn't actually attained Nirvana yet; he hadn't been kicked out like I had been.

'We'd always been close, and I couldn't believe he would leave like that – *by choice*.'

Thato was shaking her head.

'I had to rely on bursaries for school, and if Uncle Ishaan and Aunt Nadra hadn't taken me in, I don't know where I would be. I mean, what a nut job is my dad, right? And how selfish, don't you think?'

I didn't know how to respond, and my heart sank. If she thought her father was a selfish nut job, what would she make of me. A boy who closed his eyes every night to wake up in a past life. 'It's been hard on you,' I could only say.

Thato let out a humourless laugh, 'You think!' Then she shrugged. 'But I can't be angry at him. He's still my dad. I'm just... hurt.'

She jumped up after that, tossing a final fabric to one of the neat piles we'd made.

'I'm so sorry. Gosh, what on earth! I just totally spilled out my guts to you about – *everything*! Too much information! I'm embarrassed now.'

I stood up beside her. 'Hey, no, come on.' I held her hand. 'I'm glad. You trusted me enough to open up.'

She smiled. She looked closely at me.

'Gosh, you know, it's the weirdest thing, but I feel like... like...'

'We've been here many times before?' I supplied when words seemed to fail her.

'Yes!' she exclaimed. 'How is that even possible?'

I would have told her. Right there and then, spilled all my guts too. Revealed the whole quest to her and our connection through years. In full detail. Everything.

But her aunt Nadra bustled in.

'Are you two finishing, or you're just messing about,' she moaned.

'We're all done aunty,' Thato replied, quickly leading me to the door.

'Good. I'm exhausted.' Aunt Nadra said. 'Your uncle's waiting to take us home. I need a bath, food, proper rest before tomorrow. I really should take better care of myself. I do too much, you see. Always too much. I never give myself a break. And there's never anyone to help...' She carried on in that vein until Thato finished locking up the shop for the night.

As we parted, I caught sight of her Uncle Ishaan, standing by the sidewalk next to a big black SUV. He was a very tall man, with a striking regal look about him.

His face was hard and unsmiling when our eyes met. And he turned away stiffly to help his wife into the car.

I waved to Thato as they drove off, thinking it was getting late. It was almost about that time. I would try again for my own Stage One. My past was waiting.

Off of the Mediterranean Coast
(Bay of Naples)
24 October, 79AD

As suddenly as I had shut my eyes I awoke to hell. Sprayings of ash, plumes of black, suffocating smoke and tons of crashing molten rock pelting in relentless bursts. Destruction and chaos underlined by the violent shaking and breaking apart of the ground.

Instantly, my eyes, which struggled to penetrate the acidic smog were stinging, my lungs burning, painful, as I tried to gulp in air but only got sulphur. My ears throbbed with the sound of deafening rumble compounded with high pitched screams and cries to create an atmosphere of terror like I had never come across before. And the heat, not only cloying and oppressive but utterly singeing; peeling away at the skin in a slow excruciating burn.

For the briefest moment, terror struck me. My mind raced. Had I totally failed the Dharma Shastra? Was I in that awful final destination where unworthy souls went to perish forever? Was this the feared, most terrible proverbial end of the road?

Panic rising within me to the point of choking, I looked up. And, in the distance, I saw it. Tall, looming and rumbling furiously, it spewed a high-altitude column of biblical-type fire and brimstone, blanketing the entire surrounding area. Then I knew.

Mount Vesuvius was erupting. I was a citizen of Pompeii – on the last day of Pompeii's existence.

I barely had time to gather my thoughts when I was grabbed by a hand. I tore my eyes away from the erupting volcano, and the panic that had taken hold of me let go almost instantly when I looked into a pair of familiar eyes. Thato.

The mayhem seemed a distant thing; something that was happening to someone else. I could have been walking in the quiet grounds of Carbarney Manor.

She was AD Roman now – flowing white robes, gold bracelets, sandals, and with a High Priestess crescent pendant around her neck. But it was still her. The girl I'd always loved.

'Cicero!' she was yelling at me desperately, trying to be heard above the noise and chaos. 'The Ancient Artefact – in the temple – they will be coming for it. They must not get it before the end comes. They must not harness the power –'

There was a loud blast like an exploding bomb as the volcano released more large rocks. One of those rocks smashing clean across Thato's face, cutting off her words and effectively slamming her to the ground, instantly lifeless. Deep red liquid gushed everywhere.

I watched her body bleed out, stunned. In that moment I recognised the fate that we'd shared across the centuries. I'd watched her die a thousand deaths before my very own eyes. Again, and again and again. In every life, like clockwork.

Another blast ripped the air, snapping me alert.

I knew then what she'd meant about the Ancient Artefact. How I'd been a temple serving boy and how, she, Athena the High Priestess had been guarding the secret of the Ancient Artefact for so long. I knew about the powers the Artefact held; powers that had the potential to transport a soul several lives ahead – in a sense, cheat a large part of the death and rebirth cycle.

And, also, I knew of the two Shaman; twin brothers from Naples – magic practitioners and magi – who had come to know of the Artefact and who, since then, had been savagely seeking to get their hands on it. Corrupt, feckless men who would dissemble their way to any form of soul advantage.

Now, this day, Mount Vesuvius provided them a perfect opportunity. For all Athena had stood for, fire could rain hard from the heavens, but as it was just then, either way, I was determined to stop those brothers.

Running through shattering mayhem, I rushed to the temple, fighting exertion, hot ash blurring my vision and lungs brim-full of sulphur near giving out.

I made it in time to at least pounce on one of the brothers just as he made to enter the temple. Wrestling him to the ground, we became entwined in a hard brawl of flying fists and competition of strength.

But Arrius was almost an old man, and I was a strong Roman servant boy used to tough labour. I eventually overpowered him. A few well-aimed blows to the jaw left him gulping and incapable of rising.

All he could do was spit maliciously at me as I stood over him; 'You're too late, temple boy! Fabius is already in.'

Not wasting another second, dodging pulverised pumice, I went for the temple. The place was falling apart in the assault of the volcano, a right death trap. I went in anyway. Past the debris and crumbling pillars all round, I made for the sanctuary where Athena had shown me the Artefact was hidden.

Close to collapse myself, I arrived there to see Arrius's brother Fabius in front of the altar, the secret case behind it open, and he was reaching inside for the Artefact.

Knowing desperately that it was paramount that he didn't place his wicked hand in the centre, I grasped for the nearest object I could use as a weapon. A loosened ritual spire was an arm's reach away. Acting quickly, I grabbed it, hurling it at the Shaman across the space between us. The pointed end embedded in his torso. He crumpled to the ground.

I advanced as quickly as I'd thrown the spire, breathing a deep sigh of relief when I saw that the Artefact remained intact and untouched. The solid polished wood front of it gleaming, undimmed. The jewelled edges around its cross-shaped centrepiece still luminous as well.

'You made a big mistake,' the writhing Fabius now with a spire sticking out of him choked out. 'A waste. It's – going to perish –.' he struggled to speak, struggled to breathe. '– the Artefact. In the rubble – no one will ever harness its... unique powers.' He gulped blood but was relentless in getting his point across. 'It's better than Logos, you know – the man they say can lead a soul directly to Paradise.'

My ears pricked up just then. 'What?'

'Bypass the whole long, tardy process of incarnation,' the dying man replied. And this was absolute news to me. How had I never known of this man... if Fabius's pre-death rant could be believed? And why hadn't Ezer ever mentioned him; the Logos?

Catching my stunned expression, the Shaman laughed, for a moment more choking on blood, then; 'You silly ignorant boy. You don't even deserve to touch the centre of the Artefact!'

I was drawn back to the Artefact. After his taunts, I gazed at it with fresh eyes.

The cries of the frightened and wounded outside, all those people looking square into the face of certain death, filled my ears, making them ring. The ground beneath me continued to quake and the temple continued to crumble around me. It was inescapable fact: we were all done for that day.

And yet, what if there was something to this touching the centre of the Artefact business?

Time and time again, Thato had told me – well, not Thato here. Athena. Athena had told me countlessly how it was strictly forbidden to touch the centre of the Artefact. That it had a sacred purpose and that anyone who messed with it messed with universal destiny. Her one life purpose had been to guard it to ensure no one ever came close to it.

But now, I looked around and the city we'd both been born in, both grown up in, and both treasured furiously was about to get vaporised under a sea of molten lava. The Artefact would be lost forever.

I thought about what I'd remembered about Thato and me earlier. In all our lives together, I always eventually ended up watching her die. Every time. And every time as painful and soul-destroying as the last.

Standing there, a single tear burned a trail across my soot-covered cheek.

How about saving myself a bit of devastation?

Skipping a few lives ahead would spare me that awful blow of watching her die – at least for a while.

Previously when I'd lived this life before, I'd fled the scene in anxiety of saving my life somehow. Now the only thing I was eager to escape was even a fraction of terrible heartache.

Shaking with the grief of the day and the grief of days past, I stepped over the body of the now dead Shaman. I reached for the Artefact. Drawn in as if by a magnetic force, my hand went for the centre.

I touched it.

***

It proved worse than waking up to the molten hell of Pompeii. With what was like an electric current surging through every pore of me, I fell into a mad freefall. Waking up in flash after flash. Life after life. In such quick succession I barely had time to wrap my mind around a different body, place or atmosphere before it all changed again.

Rapidly, one after the other. Dizzying. And at that point, when I thought I would collapse from the overwhelming, over-powering rush... Nothing.

Perfect stillness. Perfect calm. Perfect quiet. Cautiously, I opened my eyes to find myself in a bright, white void. And, looking down at myself, I was plain SJ again. And suddenly she was there as well. Ezer. In her natural form.

Dazzling white hair; purest snow in colouring. Eyes the colour of fire; all burning red and gold. Skin like polished mahogany; deep brown and luminescent. Shimmering and misty all at once. Utterly ethereal, she approached me.

'You tried to rush things,' she said in that voice of a thousand rushing streams I remembered from what seemed very long ago. 'This is the result. Tumbling from one life to the next. Exhausting, isn't it?'

Exhausting was an understatement. I was thoroughly spent. Drained like I'd been wrung dry, body and soul.

'I can tell you,' Ezer went on. 'This is not the way to achieve virtue – or anything much else for that matter.

Did you ever consider that the Ancient Artefact was meant to melt in lava, forever untouched? Did you ever consider the destiny of that – its virtue?

It's always been essential to pace yourself SJ. Which is why a system was worked out that would allow for that. And now you find yourself caught up in this rush, making you speed through lives without even a second to fulfil any of the Dharma Shastra.'

I could hardly stand from fatigue but dug deep to find the breath to respond.

'Tell me,' I asked, breathlessly, desperately. 'Please, tell me what I can do to fix this.'

The vision that was Ezer sighed. Nonetheless, she came closer. Drew next to me in shimmering brilliance. And tenderly she touched me. I looked up at her, for the first time recognising a quality about her. Something undefinable, but as powerful as a physical grip. Something exceptionally pure and incorruptible. Something so completely heavenly.

My breath caught in my throat.

She took up my hand, the hand on which was engraved the Amulet of Atman. Gently, she began to trace with her fingers. Soft swirls appeared just above the amulet, gold in colour.

'This marking will limit the rush,' she said as she finished. 'Only somewhat, though. The floodgates have been opened and will never be entirely stemmed.

I gazed down at the fresh marking. 'And Logos?' It was a topic I had to bring up. I had to know if there was anything more at all I could do to raise my chances. 'This so-called shortcut man. Is he real? Can he really bypass all travails through multiple lives and get a soul straight to the finish line... Paradise itself? Can I find him?'

Ezer smiled enigmatically. 'Shortcut man is not the term I would use. And as for finding him; that's the heart of it all, isn't it?'

Without warning, there was another flash.

I snapped awake to the patter of morning rain on Carbarney Manor.

Chapter Four

School was a distracted blur. The voices of the teachers droned on and right over me. The press of the students between periods like phantom bodies whirling past me, intangible and unrecognised. Everything an incorporeal, shifting haze. All I could think of, all that registered, was that I'd had to watch Thato die, over and over again.

My soul was now fully awakened to that fact and overlooking it, even for a split second had become impossible. That horrible realisation I'd forgotten in the thralls of Nirvana glared fully at me now. That cause and relation between my life advancement and Thato's dying.

Each time, my advancement, my moving forward in spirit, as it were; each time was linked to – in fact, almost always *depended* on her death first. Like clockwork, she died and I advanced.

To say that this tormented me doesn't begin to describe my volcanic emotions; made that much worse by the tragedy that this pattern was set to repeat itself, in life after life; and even in the now the cycle would come full circle again.

For me to advance, for me to regain Nirvana – my whole quest's fulfilment – she would have to die.

All this a painful reel playing non-stop in my mine, at football practise after lessons, I saw her. Heading up onto the field with the girls' team for a warmup session for their own club practise. She looked up, caught me watching and smiled, eyes glinting playfully. I smiled back.

I knew how little time I would have with her here. And I wanted nothing more than to make the most of it. This time we didn't have a lifetime to get to know each other. The one life a night task, the hundred and ten lives – a century and a decade – it had meant only about three and a half months in present time. But that three and a half months was probably even less now with this freefall route I'd started, whizzing through multiple lives on any given night. It meant less time here, in the now. Less time with Thato.

With each passing second, we were closer to separation. With each passing second, she was closer to death.

Knocking me out of my gloom, a heavy whack across the face set my head throbbing. I'd been hit with a football. The bustling activity of the field around me suddenly became fully formed again. Patrick was laughing.

'Pay attention Hudson!' he yelled. 'Pass the ball. The ball SJ – pass the ball!'

I passed the ball. Patrick took the shot on goal. It canon-balled right to the back of the net. Immediately, he was running, arms flailing, coming to jump excitedly on me.

'Wu! Did you see that? Bam! Like zero help from you but still made it elegant. Come on mate, where's your head at? Chop-chop!' he urged. 'Here we go.'

Running quickly to keep up with him, I made to follow him into the thick of the game.

Then there was another boy running beside me. Close. Too close.

'You seem troubled, *Ladaka*.'

I did a double take before shaking my head. 'Not now Ezer,' I responded coldly. 'I have a game to finish.' Trotting further towards centre field, I distanced myself.

Ezer was last on my list of conversation that day. All along she'd known about Thato; hadn't bothered preparing me, or even just giving me a heads up. What kind of guardian – what kind of "helper" – was that?

I didn't want to talk to her. Most certainly didn't want any of her moral rationales right now.

The only one I wanted, the only one I needed was Thato. And as soon as her practise session ended, I was off the pitch, not caring that both Patrick and the coach were yelling after me. Before she made it to the changing rooms, I stopped her.

'Hey! You wanna get a milkshake or something?' I jumped right in with.

Mopping up her damp brow with a towel, Thato smiled. 'Wouldn't mind actually, but I still have drama club. In –' she flicked a wristwatch, '– ten minutes. Which means, I'm already late! Thanks for the thought though.'

She was about to brush past me. Quickly, I added, 'Need a walking buddy then?' I knew I was coming on strong, but I didn't care. 'I was actually on my way –'

Thato laughed. Lightly, she put a hand to my arm. 'Ease up SJ. Don't worry, I'll see you around.' A small wave and she'd gone to re-join a group of girls heading to the changing rooms.

I was left standing at the edge of the field, the tattoo on my palm throbbing like an unsubtle reminder.

~

I showed up to drama club. Without invite and without really any plan for a way forward. I just needed to be where she was. On stage in the school's main hall, flanked by her fellow actors, her teeth showed dazzling white, contrasting beautifully with the smooth darkness of the face they were set in, as she laughed, watching my approach through the aisles.

'Room for one more?' I asked, my voice booming through the auditorium.

'Always,' she replied, eyes lighting up. 'Come on up SJ. Now, guys, auditions for *Arcadia* are coming up next week, and I have some great news. Mrs. Owens says it will be staged this mid-term at Carbarney Castle's Oats Theatre!'

The place erupted with exclamations of glee, hugs and high-fives. This was obviously a big deal for the Carbarney College drama club. Merging with the actors, I could only dig my hands deeper into my jeans pockets and smile lightly in feigned solidarity.

'Yes, fantastic news,' Thato went on. 'The Annual play's really going to be amazing this year. And Mrs. Owens will be joining us later on this session, but I'll help get things going in the meantime. Grab some chairs. I'll hand out the material and we can begin.'

I followed cue, already counting down the minutes to a break. And forty-five minutes later when there finally was one, I was at Thato's side once again, repeating my milkshake offer.

She was gracious as ever but suggested a rain check yet again. 'I have a super important dinner-meeting with the Dean of Science and some of the other heads of departments. I'll be the student perspective,' she mock-grimaced. 'And I know your follow-up question, and the answer is, no – I never stop. I have like forty-five billion commitments!'

I couldn't help a small laugh. 'Wow, yeah. I'm starting to get that. Can't be easy being Head Prefect, I imagine.'

'Ag, no, it's not. But, hey, don't feel sorry for me; I love it! Live for the responsibility.'

'And power,' I joked.

She shrugged it off. 'Please, as if anyone ever really listens to me anyway.'

She was smiling. I was smiling back at her. Whatever was between us, just then, she felt it too. I may have been the only one who remembered the full extent of it, but there was no denying that she felt it too.

'Alright gang,' it was Mrs. Owens breezing into the auditorium. 'What did I miss?'

The spell between us was interrupted, but not broken. And I knew what I had to do. Trying to get time with Thato was looking as good as trying for an audience with the Pope. She was so driven, so spread out over so many responsibilities and commitments that the only way I would ever have any hope of making any headway with her was if I became part of those commitments.

So, wholeheartedly, I threw myself into the drama club. Even auditioning for the mid-term play. And when I got a minor part in it, I threw myself into that as well. It didn't matter that come midterm my soul would have probably moved on. What I thought of was Thato's soul, and the time left on her own cycle. This play gave us the time we would otherwise not have had.

I was already playing multiple characters every night of every day in different past lives, what was one more persona to assume during the day? If it got me closer to my soulmate; closer to figuring out how to cheat death and make us last, then I would without doubt give it everything I had.

Which I did. Being at every rehearsal. Costume fittings and the endless running of lines. And when we took our sessions from the school auditorium to Carbarney Castle itself, I was one of the first ones there. Always with her. Thato. I was growing to enjoy the rehearsal sessions, the excitement, fun and unavoidable drama of stage production. But more than that the closeness with my one reason for being there in the first place.

But as our connection and friendship deepened, so did the overwhelming burden of knowing the link of our fate. And Ezer was never far off, in the background or outrightly accosting me. I couldn't listen to her – wouldn't listen – being so caught up in that bubble of my own suffering; that poignancy of my limited time with the girl I'd known for centuries.

'You'll help bring in the rest of the props?' Thato said to me as we got out of the drama club van. Mrs. Owens was sliding out the driver's seat and the rest of the club were shuffling out as well.

The stone and concrete majesty that was Carbarney Castle rose up in front of us. An old, historic building with a history that stretched to the Plantagenet era. It brought up memories for me.

But to Thato I only nodded. 'Yep. Sure.' Heading towards the back of the van to help some other lads with the heavy bags.

The castle was an imposing centre piece in an expansive parkland. Of grey brick and mortar, it stood tall, looming as if it meant to touch the cloudy sky; all heavy columns and weathered stone. A magnificent piece of medieval architecture. And no doubt with many stories it could tell of the goings-on of lives lived and passed within its walls.

Inside was preserved and displayed all its wealth of aged artefacts. Patterns and designs; furniture and drapes; outdated but having far outlived those who'd made them, bought them, used them.

'Are you coming, dawdle duck?' Thato teased. She was standing in an archway, her backdrop the old elegance around us. I suddenly saw her in medieval clothes. Curly, red hair packed haphazardly into a white cape; a white apron round her waist.

There was a time she'd been a maid in a place like this.

I blinked. Picked up speed to catch up with her, and we went into the theatre area together. A massive space that seemed a separate building of its own, seeming independent of the rest of the castle. Here it was remodelled, refurnished with every contemporary convenience and equipment.

'It's awesome, isn't it?' Thato said close beside me. She clapped her hands together excitedly. 'I can't wait to stage our production here!'

I put down the equipment I'd been lugging, turning to share in her enthusiasm. Trying not to think about the fact that in all likelihood neither she nor I would be around for the production. The moving on of our souls in whatever way – for better or for worse – was inevitable.

Rehearsals were standard, running smoothing. Everyone was keen and excited to be at the Oates. Thato lovely and cheekily playful as always. I was almost forgetting our tragedy, almost near to enjoying myself as well, when mid-way through practise there was a visitor.

The Brahmin, i.e. High Priest of the local Hindu temple, Ishaan Farouk. Thato's uncle.

Hard-faced as ever, he stood tall and imposing by the entrance, his traditional, bright-coloured priestly robes still casting a shadow for all their brilliance. Dark-haired with chiselled features, he was as striking as I remembered; the top of a tattoo on his chest just visible above his open collar. The crown of what appeared to be the head of the deity Shiva; the destroyer.

Immediately, Thato excused herself. They stepped out into the hallway together. She was gone a while. And when she came back, a little of her usual lustre was lost. She made her apologies to Mrs. Owens, and with a small wave to me, headed out.

Not caring that I was in the middle of an important scene, I went after her, stopping her in one of the corridors.

'I have to go, SJ. My uncle's waiting,' she said softly.

'But why? What's happened? Why do you have to leave right now?'

'It's nothing. Just my aunt and the shop. Bye SJ.'

I took her arm before she could turn away. 'Thato –'

'SJ, *please*,' she was snappy now. 'Just drop it. You don't have to be in all my business *all* the time! Stop acting like you know my life. You're just a guy from school. You don't know anything. Back off!' She yanked out of my light grasp, storming off without giving me the slightest chance for response.

~

Grandpa Smitty was waiting for me when I got home. Striding from his sitting room into the hallway as soon as he heard the door.

Scraggy white eyebrows joined together in a frown, he boomed, 'At last! Dear boy, I don't believe I've set eyes on you this entire week. It's near living with a ghost.'

I sighed, hanging up my coat. I didn't say that, yes, in fact, I was a ghost. A lost soul, trapped between times. And that the only person who made any of it make sense, or any of it even worth it probably resented me right now and wanted nothing more to do with me.

'Hey Papa,' I said instead. 'Did you go alright with the goose hunt today?' Or was that pheasant or deer or some other game?

'Pheasant, dear boy. We were at the pheasants this afternoon.'

Ah. Pheasants. I never could keep up with the hunting enthusiasms of my aristocratic grandfather. Just then I felt a pang for my Bohemian parents. It didn't last long though.

How many souls had I called mother and father over the decades? How many grandfathers – grandmothers had I had?

Dozens upon dozens, and each adding and enriching with some value to my own existence and the gradation of my soul.

I was here, with Grandpa Smitty for a reason.

'You have become so occupied with that drama business,' he went on gruffly. 'Even your parents are starting to wonder about what's going on with you. And you missed our fishing last week...'

I decided to give him a break.

'Sorry Papa. I promise, this week I'll be there. You won't need to remind me or ask me twice.'

This seemed to mollify him a bit. We went in to supper together. Tonight, he'd made sure to hold off the meal till I got back, and we could dine together.

Filled up with anxieties and sadness, I wasn't very hungry, buts to placate Grandpa Smitty made an effort with what the chef had laid out.

In between courses, my eyes were constantly drawn to the clock.

I wondered what the night held in store for me. Would I achieve Dharma? And in that case, where would that leave Thato? Would we ever meet up in Nirvana?

Or would I have yet another failure, eluded by virtue once again and wake up to another cold morning to begin another day in a life ticking away much too quickly?

'Eat up, my boy,' Grandpa Smitty urged, catching my drifting mind. 'Need to keep up the strength.'

Picking up my fork and knife again, I thought to myself; *You have no idea, Papa; the herculean amount of strength I am going to need.*

Chapter Five

But dawn came far too soon. I opened my eyes and after tumbling through a fire-shot of former lives, I was still none the closer to any Dharma Shastra. Disheartenment took hold like a tight, gripping cloak around me that showed no hope of ever letting go.

I found I didn't have the strength to muddle through another ordinary day at Carbarney College. All I could do was linger in bed, watching the constant patter of rain at my window. Then the most I mustered after that was heading to the games room, losing myself in a succession of PlayStation games; barely getting midway through one before moving on to the next.

But when the afternoon seemed to stretch more void than my morning had been, I thought about drama practise. In an hour or so the club would be meeting like clockwork at Carbarney Castle. I contemplated going. Talked myself in and out, before drawing up a mental image of the four lives I'd been in last night; a mental image that had a common thread – Thato, always Thato; and the endings… always the endings.

I got up quickly to shower and get dressed.

It was still lightly raining when I got to the Castle. Not keen to meet up with anyone up front, also to have that much longer to steady my own thoughts and turmoil, I took the long route through the gardens. I wished I hadn't when a groundsman I hadn't seen come up from the hedging suddenly was in front of me.

'You don't have to be alone in this, *Ladaka*,' he said.

It was Ezer. Immediately, a little petulantly, I turned away.

'I told you I don't want to talk, Ezer,' I snapped.

'We don't have to talk,' she was in stride beside me. 'I just want you to know that I'm here. I'll always be. And if you need me, I am that support. You only have to choose it, *Ladaka*. I don't force myself on anyone.'

The retort bubbling on the tip of my tongue was choked down as she pulled back. The groundsman carried on about his work.

'SJ?'

I jumped a little, turning to see Thato standing there, umbrella held up against the rain.

'Hi – Thato! I was just on my way to the Oates. Thought I'd take the scenic route,' I smiled sheepishly.

'Well, come on then. And there's plenty room under here,' she offered the shelter of the wide umbrella.

I ducked under with her in spite being already sodden. We walked steadily.

'Listen. I'm sorry about the other day,' she began.

Almost immediately, I waved it off. 'No. Come on, don't worry about it. I get it.'

'No. No. I should apologise. And I want to. You were only trying to help, and I was incredibly rude. Truth be told I was more frustrated at my uncle than you. It was easy to lash out at you rather than him. He was just coming down on me a bit hard about my multitude of extracurricular. Doesn't really get the whole Head Prefect thing and the obligations and so on. All he hears is my Aunt Nadra whining on about how she has the burden of the shop all to herself, and how they never see me. Like living with a phantom!'

I snorted. 'My Grandad said the exact same thing to me yesterday.'

'Yeah? Gosh, how's that hey. I suppose he misses you more than anything else, right? You don't have some shop in the woodworks that he needs you to help run.'

'No. Geez. Yeah. He's like most parents, I guess. Wants to be more involved; connect more.'

'Well, it's not like that with my family. I wish it was – it isn't though. It's just... It's just so complex with us... Uncle Ishaan and Aunt Nadra never had kids, and when my dad left to pursue his whole Moksha thing, I guess they felt as if they couldn't say no, you know, when he asked them to take me in. I mean, my uncle being of the "great priestly" class of the Brahmin and heading the performing of the religious rites at the temple. He could have never been seen to say no. And in the beginning, my father's money mollified them a bit, sweetened things along. But when he gave all that away to charity for his Samnyasa that made things a bit rocky.

I mean, Aunt Nadra's harmless enough, she just wants help with the shop, but Uncle Ishaan... I don't know about him sometimes. There's a lot of resentment bubbling under the surface, I feel – towards Dad; towards me... I don't know.' She shrugged.

We were just outside of the Castle now. I wanted to hug her. Instead, I offered my hand. Surprisingly, she took it. We stood for a minute like that, just holding hands. Me just as much giving comfort as receiving it.

'So, everything's cool with your grandad now?' she asked eventually, dropping her hand from mine as we carried on walking.

'Yeah,' I replied. 'I basically apologised and promised not to disappoint him for our weekly fishing jaunt coming up.'

'Oh, my gosh, fishing!' Thato brightened.

I frowned. 'No. Don't tell me you're into it too? Honestly, I'm not mad about it, and I just go for Grandpa Smitty's sake!'

'Well, I don't think I'm anywhere near the enthusiast your Grandad is, but my Dad used to take me, and I find it good fun, actually.'

I laughed. 'That's surprising. Never would've pegged you for a... fishing girl.'

'Hm, I am rather. Are tag-alongs welcome at this weekly event or is it strictly a Grandad-grandson moment.'

'I don't know about the strictly bit, but Grandpa Smitty tends to be happy with anyone who shares any of his outdoor passions.'

'So, is that an invitation?' Thato stopped.

I followed suit. 'Totally, yeah – if you're into that type of torture!'

'Cool! So, it's a date then.'

Her cheeky grin; the sparkle in her eyes as she said that. I was reminded again of why I'd fallen for her without fail hundreds of times over hundreds of years.

Grandpa Smitty was in fact just short of deliriously thrilled to have someone else to share the many joys of fishing – as he called them – and to impart the extensive, pearls-of-wisdom knowledge he had on the subject – again according to his own words.

I was thankful to see that Thato took his, at times, over-keenness in stride. She was the appropriately deferring student and eager fishing partner. I may as well have not been there at all, they seemed to get on so well.

Becoming more a side-line spectator, by the edge of the manor lake, a little way off from where they stood, as they talked angling and tried out different baiting techniques. I didn't mind watching though. I tried to just savour the moment. The weather mellow; a light autumn breeze rustling golden-brown leaves, and a pale sun peeking out from behind the clustered grey puffs of clouds. Each second I took as precious.

But, at the end of it, I knew I had to fully open up to her. She'd left nothing of herself hidden from me. She'd opened up about her life, her struggles and inner turmoil. Deep down, it had always been imperative that I do the same. We'd been together for centuries. This was as much her story as it was mine. And, anyway, it was crushing me, bearing everything alone. More than Ezer; more than anyone, she would most understand.

As soon as the last fish of the day was caught, and we were packing up to return to the Manor, I inched closer to her, out of hearing shot of Grandpa Smitty who was studiously sorting fish in a cooler box.

'There's something I want to show you,' I said softly.

She took in my tone and my whole expression as I said that. Her brows came together a little. 'Okay. It sounds serious.'

I didn't add to the sudden heaviness between us with the dramatic response of *It's a matter of life and death*, but I guess my expression said it all because she stopped her final packing and faced me fully with a quizzical look.

'Let's finish off here, and we can go? It's not really something I can tell. It's more something I have to show you.'

✳✳✳

Night had fallen. A single, shaded corner lamp gave a light glow to the bedroom. The many drapes were drawn and there was keen intimacy about the setting.

Bellies full of a large fish supper, we sat together on the bed. Trust and closeness that went beyond the space between us. Thato wasn't nervous. Neither was I, come to think of it. For the first time since being here, it wasn't with heart-in-throat dread that I anticipated what was coming. With Thato here with me it seemed so much less daunting.

She didn't object when I gently laid her back onto the pillows and soon after took up position beside her. My righthand side by with her left hand.

'Okay. So where is this mysterious spectacle you want to show me,' she asked softly. Then half joking, 'You're not trying to get lucky here, are you? I know I'm an older woman but I'm not that sort of girl Lord Carbarney.'

I chuckled gently. 'Firstly, Lord Carbarney is my grandfather. And as hard as it for your liberal mind to wrap around, I'm an heir to an heir – not *the* heir. Secondly, two teen years does not make you an "older woman". Anyway, age is relative in the soul realm. And last, but not least, you should be so lucky!'

Thato gasped at that, laughed and hit me in the arm playfully. 'Oh, just get on with this thing of yours. I'm bored already!'

I felt the bantering mood drain away. I looked at her seriously. 'Brace yourself. You're going to have bit of a shock. Are you ready?'

'Yes,' she whispered, a little breathlessly.

'Close your eyes.'

70

Both our eyes shut, I slowly linked our hands. My palm against her palm. Heat began to radiate from the amulet, searing us both, and we were transported in a snap.

We opened our eyes to dense jungle. Thickest, wild foliage with rays of brilliant hot sun slicing through the rich greenery. The earth was moist and rich beneath our bare feet. The air warm and pure around us.

'What in the world...' She was gazing about in unadulterated wonder. 'SJ, where are we...' But when she turned to look at me, she jumped. The wonder in her eyes turned to fright. She took in the animal cloth around my waist, my deep chestnut, muscled body and long, straight dark hair. The tattoos covering my skin; the bone piercing my nostrils. She scampered back, stunned. 'What? Where's SJ? Who are you...? What...?'

'Thato. It's me. It's still me.' I tried to advance, she retreated even further, her bare chest rapidly rising and falling with panic.

'No. You're not – this isn't...' she looked around again, then back at me, then down at herself. A loud yelp as she quickly brought her hands up to cover her chest, realising that the only thing she also wore was the fragmentary skin cloth around the waist. Then another yelp as she took in the colour of those hands – the colour of her whole body in fact. Her limbs, her hair, the feel of her face; it was all different.

She screamed. Loud. Piercing. Over and over again. Hysterically.

I tried to get a hold of her. Quieten her down but she only fought me.

Eventually, she screamed and scrambled us both back to Carbarney. Instantly jumping off the bed we'd been lying on.

'Oh my gosh. O my gosh!' She touched her hands, her arms, her chest; rushed for the full-length mirror by the wardrobe. Purest relief washed over her when she saw her reflection. Tall, slim, mahogany... Herself again.

That's when she turned to me. She rushed back to where I now sat on the bed.

'SJ. What in the HELL was that?' Eyes wide as saucers.

I took a deep breath. 'Not hell, Thato... *life*. Our life. A previous life.'

She blinked. 'What?'

'Okay,' I began. 'You wanna sit down for this?' I indicated the same space next to me she'd been on only moments ago.

'Ah, no. No way,' she shook her head. 'I'm going to stand right here, thank you very much!'

'Totally get that.' I nodded. 'Right. So... Where to begin...'

She was looking at me expectantly, impatiently; desperate to have the insanity that had just passed explained.

I took another deep breath, releasing it slowly.

'You know Moksha, right?'

She blinked. Then again, several more times, as if clearing her brain and having to re-gather her thoughts after what had just happened.

'Uhm, yeah. That's my dad's whole crazy trip. His whole mad thing is based on attaining this... Moksha. Don't tell me now it's not craziness after all! And what's worse is that what I just saw, where I was like two seconds ago is even crazier than my dad's whole ten-year madness!'

'There is no craziness, Thato.' I said quietly. 'Moksha is very much real.'

She went very still. Rendered immobile as well as speechless.

'And you know what comes after Moksha? Nirvana. But, get this, though; Nirvana is not just a... *state*... of supreme happiness or whatever. It's an actual place. Like a stepover before true Paradise – or what some would call Heaven.

The souls in Nirvana don't know it when they arrive but it's essentially the ultimate qualifying round. Existing in a state of perpetual bliss, do you still maintain having what it takes for Paradise itself?

In life it's a test of; can you survive turmoil and hardship. In Nirvana it's a question of; how do you handle perfection? Do you stay true and virtuous or do you stumble and fall and get back to square one?

I was there – Nirvana. Enough to say, I didn't make the cut.'

Thato, of her own volition this time, sank onto the bed beside me. Bemused and struck all at once. Her gaze urged me to continue.

'Well, now to get back to Nirvana I've been granted a hundred and ten lives out of my existence to fulfil the whole Dharma Shastra. With this...' I held up the amulet etched on my palm. '... Every night I go back. Dharma, Artha, and Kama. These are the three Shastra I have to attain to be able to go back to Nirvana. I'm not even done with the first one, and I've gone through dozens of lives already. And if my hundred and ten run out and I still have nothing...' The thought of it chilled me to a pause.

'What? What SJ? What happens?' Such was her genuine worry for me; touching.

I sighed. 'I'm lost. Forever.'

'Wow.' A hand fixed to her mouth as she tried to fully digest the scope of it all. 'Wow,' she breathed again. Her other hand reached for me, coming to rest on my arm. Then both hands were on my arm.

'I can't even begin to imagine what it must be like for you. To know... and to have to travel... It's... mad. But you're strong SJ. So strong and resilient. It's funny, I haven't known you that long, but I just feel this so strongly about you. You have all the capability to smash the whole Shastra thing. You can do this. I know you can.'

Tears stung my eyes. I was moved. I wanted to tell her that she knew me – better than anyone in hundreds of years had ever known me, and that her words meant the world to me because of that. But then I thought, like with my Shastra, some things you can't just tell, somethings you just have to show.

'Gosh,' she choked back tears of her own. 'I can't believe though that, in a sense, you were kicked out of heaven. Like, mate, how bad were you – how bad does someone have to be to be kicked out of heaven!'

We both laughed. It dispersed a lot of the heaviness, and I felt more motivated than I'd been since I first arrived.

'So, what do you say?' I asked. 'Should we try that again? Thato Elaine Singh, do you want to go back to another life with me?'

Slowly, she smiled and nodded. The magnetism between us was undeniable; inextinguishable.

We lay back down again.

II

The Xiango Empire
185BC

A full-blown riotous celebration. And I found myself right in the thicket of it. Swathes of shimmering robes billowing around me. Brightly coloured, luminous lanterns lighting up a flurry of confetti and floating ribbons. More drink and food than any one place could contain, and even more people – boldly and extravagantly attired Chinese nobles – consuming both drink and food, while laughing, talking and dancing to the background music of traditional *yayue*.

Happy chaos I was at once separated from, realising almost immediately that Thato was not with me. We'd definitely travelled back together – I was sure of that; had felt it as our souls meshed in transporting. But she was nowhere in sight. And among the throng, I battled to see anything even a metre away, much less spot her.

As I turned, trying to scan the area more, a young man approached me. He was dressed in the Jiang clan servant garments; tunic and slacks, all in grey. He bowed low to me and called me Master. It came to me then who I was and where I was.

The manservant was going on about important clan leaders who wanted to meet me, and how he'd been tasked to take me to them. I barely paid attention. My thoughts were wholly fixated on finding Thato.

I brushed past the still talking Jiang, almost shoving through the throng now. But I didn't get very far before another man stopped me. A red-faced, pot-bellied nobleman who was drunk beyond his limits. He actually half toppled onto me as he accosted me.

I had to help steady him with both hands. He laughed raucously in my face.

'So, here you are!' he yelled. 'The Great Zin-Long of the Zhou clan. What a pity, ehy. Such a pity. As Samurai commander of Zhou, it's you whose wedding we're supposed to be celebrating here. You who was always meant to marry the Princess. Nasty thing she did to you. Everyone thinks so. Pities you. I mean, to discard you – an imperial commander and Prince! – to wed a mere low-raking soldier. Madness, pure madness.'

I humoured him by nodding agreement, all the while trying to be free of him. But he clung to me even tighter.

'Everyone is enraged for you, you know. Everyone! And there're even factions – yes, certain factions so angered by the Princess's decision that there's... "talk" – if you know what I mean. Some say rather than this shame on our crown and our society, maybe it's best if she were dead...'

Here the drunken noble was roughly pulled back. Another Over Lord came in the conversation, and sternly muted any further talk on the subject,

'Enough of such speculation, Chou!' he said firmly. 'Clearly too much wine muddles your brain, good man, and makes you reckless in speech.'

I looked up at him, knowing him instantly. His dark eyes gazed hard at me.

'Now, come away. The night holds still more wonders. Away, and let Master Zin-long alone to enjoy himself. Come.'

The final gleam in his look as he led off the drunken Chou told me what I needed to know. It was him. Ling-Wu. Had been him all along. He was the main voice behind these "angered factions"; the main driving force of the discontent and plotting. And he was the one who'd kill the Princess tonight.

Violently now, I pushed through bodies.

Where was she? Where was Thato.

Just as my frustration threatened to get the better of me, a few people in front of me suddenly shifted, creating a gap where I could glimpse the high table, the bridal table of honour.

And there she was.

Beautiful and resplendent in traditional marriage attire: a true princess of one of the greatest Chinese clans.

She should have been beaming, happy and smiling at this her wedding feast. But the gleaming; the smiling, laughter and happiness were all with those around her. She shared none of it. Sitting perched, almost at the edge of her elaborate bridal seat, she was stiff and sharply straight; delicate facial features marred by disorientation and confusion.

This was our reality here.

We'd been betrothed since we were children, but we'd never met; our respective kingdoms so far apart. The alliance had been struck by others on our behalf. We were meant to meet and wed when we both came of age. That had been the plan. A plan that never saw fruition, because my betrothed had grown up to be a rebellious young woman.

Jaded by the politics of royalty and stifled by its customs, she'd been like a tethered head-strong mare, biting hard against the bit that restrained her.

And when one of her father's – the Emperor's – young guards came along offering an alternative life to the one she'd grown to resent so much, she'd all but jumped at being with him. She would marry him and renounce her throne. Finally, be free.

She hadn't wanted to entertain even the thought of meeting her aristocrat fiancé. She'd not even set eyes on him... on me.

And that had been our destiny. To not meet until the day of her wedding to another man.

She looked up just then, seeing me in the crowd. Our eyes met and locked.

Yes; our destiny to meet now, when it was too late.

Her eyes grew wide. In an instance she both recognised me and realised her colossal mistake. Immediately, she stood to make a move towards me.

That's when I caught sight of it. A glinting blade in the folds of the commander Ling-Wo's robes. And his stealthy attempts to conceal it as he advanced towards her.

Quickly, I circumvented crowd, rushing for the Princess.

Reaching her a fraction of a second before the commander, and, without thought, without pause or the slightest hesitation, I lunged myself in front of her, just as the blade was thrust.

But the piercing sink of it never came. Despite my efforts, the blade had found its mark already. She bled.

As people screamed and commotion ensued, the Princess sank to the ground. I barely caught her before she hit the bed of confetti and ribbons beneath us. Distraught, I clung to her profusely bleeding body.

Not far off, the Emperor's guard were apprehending a maniacal Ling-Wo. Others of the guard tried to force me away from their assassinated royal. I would not let her go. I fought them off – one against several – as hard as I could, until one of them landed the backend of a sword to my forehead.

Blackness overcame me, my tears awash on Thato's deathly cold face.

Our souls careened once more.

Ulundi, Zululand
1879

The Anglo-Zulu war had been raging for months. I was a soldier in the British Army, she was a Zulu medicine woman and one of the fiercest warriors of her clan. We'd become unlikely friends at an unlikely time as both sides initially sent representatives either way to try and smooth over delicate relations. An advanced student of the English language, she stood for her clans' people, and I, a soldier and an experienced negotiator, stood for mine.

We'd spoken at length. Meeting after meeting. Coming to recognise our kindred spirits, and how, when it all came down to it, the last thing either of our sides needed was war.

Yet, here we were. Meeting once more – for a last time – on the battlefield of Ulundi. Ever on opposing sides.

Negotiations had irretrievably broken down – not between us, but between those above us. Men who called the shots, made the rules. Men who would stop at nothing until the red alluvial soils of this magnificent Zulu kingdom were even redder with flowing hot blood.

My war mission just then? Nirvana and the Dharma Shastra? They were the furthest things from my mind that sun-scorched July afternoon. As in the life before, as ever, I needed to find the Warrior Woman. I needed to find Thato.

I had no more appetite for fighting. No more appetite for defending and honouring Queen and Country. I just wanted out... with her.

In the thicket of bows and arrows, guns and mutilated bodies, I trudged, desperate for a glimpse of the tall, statuesque woman I had come to know.

It was nothing short of divinity when I saw her. Charging at one of my compatriots, shield and spear poised, she was all drive and rage. She would have had him, pierced clean in the chest with her spear, but then she saw me. Saw me and stopped short instantly, like a figurine suddenly frozen.

The Pith Helmet she'd been on the verge of stabbing gathered himself and picked up his gun to fight back.

'Look out!' I yelled.

One of Thato's own compatriots managed to trip the man up. But as he fell to the ground, the Pith man's weapon discharged almost of its own accord.

A careening bullet lodged in Thato's chest.

She went down.

I didn't get within ten feet of where she'd fallen. A spear was lodged in my back.

Another life followed on the heels of another darkness.

Then the same mantra, on repeat: complication and death. Her death.

Again.
Complication and death.
Her death.

Again.

Complication and death.
Her death.
In rapid succession.
Till a final gasp and we were awake.

Chapter Six

The first rays of morning light filtering in through the windows, we held on to each other, as if letting go would see us spiral down again into endless abysses of time where we had no control over the distances or circumstances that would divide us.

A little longer and we separated slowly.

I looked at Thato. She looked at me.

She said;

'That's why. I didn't know why before – these past months. Now I know. I know why I've been so drawn to you from the very first. This... you and me... across centuries... this is why.'

I didn't need to affirm her words. I only elaborated.

'You may have heard of a "soul-tie". Where souls are... aligned or joined together – sometimes even through millennia. Whichever souls knew each other, or bonded, are attracted to each other, over and over again. Some soul-ties can be broken – easily. Some, not so easily. Our soul-tie is a unique one. It goes deeper, is stronger than most...'

A smile touched her lips as the truth of that sank in. But the smile quickly fell, and a shadow seemed to pass across her delicate face. Something occurred to her just then.

'Every time... before, when we travelled, you tried to save me. And each time you couldn't...'

The breath caught in my chest.

'...It's happened consistently, hasn't it?' her tone was subdued. 'In all our lives together, we never make it all the way together, do we? I... die.'

It almost hurt to breathe; I became so choked up. I could only nod. Then forcing myself to recover, I added quickly,

'But there's a man – this supreme being they call Logos. They say he has the ability to transcend a soul straight to Paradise. A supreme and powerful being. And if he actually does have such powers, he *can* help us. We just have to find him – through the lives. He's there – maybe even *here* – I know it! And he can make things right so that we never have to be parted again.'

Tears shone in her eyes, but she braved another small smile. 'You really believe that?'

I grasped her hands in mine, looked at her in earnest. 'With all my heart.' It was firm declaration I truly stood by. 'Our souls will be set free, Thato – if nothing else, I promise you that. I'll do whatever it takes but we'll be free – both of us.'

I stood by my declaration. I stood by this promise. The nature of my mission had changed. The stakes were higher than ever now.

~

At the college, I was with Patrick in the main quad during breaktime, trying to keep up with his impassioned updates on the latest sporting results when I met up with Thato again. Well, actually, she came to me, walking with purposeful strides, exceptionally decorated blazer flapping in the wind.

At first, Patrick stepped up, thinking she'd come for him. She smiled politely at him but came to stand with me.

'Hi,' she said softly.

'Hi,' I replied. And with the barely subtle chemistry between us, Patrick was left gaping a little in surprise.

'Can you meet me?' Thato went on 'Later – after school...'

'At drama club?' I asked.

'No. Before.' She replied. 'Maybe in the Remembrance Garden? I really need to talk to you.'

'Yeah. Sure. Just say the time and I'll be there.'

She seemed anxious and I was immediately worried. As I watched her leave after she confirmed the time of our rendezvous, I knew I would be on tenterhooks the rest of the school day, wondering what was up. Beside me Patrick let out a half chuckle, half scoff.

'And since when are you and *Mein Führer* over there buddy buddy?' he was incredulous. 'It's a crazy world! You going up this way to class?'

'Yeah.'

'I'll come with,' he said.

'Cool,' I grabbed my bits, making to follow him.

'Tread carefully along this path, *Ladaka*.'

I stopped short. 'What?'

Patrick turned back to me. 'What, what?'

'You. You said something just now...'

He was looking at me blankly, and the lights came on in my head. Ezer.

Tread carefully along this path.

She obviously meant with me involving Thato so much in my travelling. Thato who was my only link to sanity in this increasingly impossible mission. Of course, I would "tread carefully". It meant life and death for the girl I loved. Life and death for me. Ezer didn't need to butt in with her pockets of stating the obvious.

I would meet Thato in the Remembrance Garden later on. We would work this out together. It was our only hope.

~

The World War II Remembrance garden sat in the middle of the school grounds. A wide, perfectly landscaped expanse of thick greenery and lush flowers. Stone benches strategically scattered around the centrepiece, a tall and elaborate water fountain.

Thato was waiting for me by the fountain. Together we perched on its granite edge.

'There's something I want to show you,' she said.

I readied myself.

She rolled up the sleeves of an arm and opened her left palm. A faint outline of the amulet I had on my own hand had been etched onto hers.

My breath caught somewhat. Having her travel with me; pressing hands to link us in those soul-journeys, it was literally leaving its mark on her.

'And that's not all,' she went on. 'I'm starting to remember things... to recognise things SJ...'

I sat up. 'What things?'

Thato sighed. 'Like when I got home this morning. I was getting ready for school. And –' Here she seemed at a loss for words. Then; 'I have a picture of my dad, by my bedside. It's of him and me when I was little. And how's this, I knew him. Like *knew* him, not just from now, being my dad. I knew him from times past. I remember him SJ. Remember him from so many lives before this. He's always been there.

Not always as my dad. Sometimes he's been a friend or co-worker or someone I know from the community. But always he's been there for me. He's always helped me somehow – like in this life he took me from where I had no one; adopted me; took care of me; loved me!'

'You have a soul-tie with him.' It was clear. 'Different than ours but, still, his soul and yours have been connected. A soul father-daughter tie.'

'I knew it!' Thato slapped a hand to the granite she sat on. 'And all these realisations just flooded through my mind. About all he's meant to me along the line. About his own soul trials and yearnings. He's been working for Nirvana like you, you know. In every life; through history. It's been his one, goal. And he's suffered so much SJ. I know you've suffered too – still suffer! – but, SJ, Veda has been his existence – every time, every life.

I just understand so much now. His whole drive for Moksha; leaving and disappearing into Samnyasa. It all makes so much sense to me right now. And I just feel such compassion for him. I've had my own journeys, but they've been nowhere near as dedicated and heart-breaking as Dad's. Every single time, he's tried so hard, given his life, and continuously failed.'

I could relate to that. I was no closer to any of the Dharam Shastra myself. But I also recognised the depth of Farhan's pursuit and that heartache of it that Thato spoke of. I'd only now been conscious of the Dharma Shastra. Only now actively working to gain them. For souls like Farhan, souls like the twin brothers I'd left to burn in Pompeii – Arrius and Fabius – for those souls, it was something they'd been acutely conscious of from an early age and had been striving towards for millennia upon millennia.

I could understand Thato's compassion for her father. I felt it for him too. Not for the brothers, who were inherently wicked souls trying to cheat their way to Nirvana. But for Farhan I did. He was a genuine soul who just couldn't seem to get there.

Thato and I spoke more. I mostly listened, though, as she outlined some of the stories she remembered her and Farhan sharing in times past. It was good to see her eyes sparkle and hear her laugh at one or the other funny situations that had passed.

For the moment we didn't say much about the faint outline of the Amulet of Atman on her left palm. She seemed grateful for this awakening and didn't want to overthink possessing the amulet and what that could mean for her own journey. And Ezer's latest words of warning still ringing in my ears, I wasn't too keen on dwelling on it myself.

At the end of it, it seemed natural that I ask her if she'd be round again that night. And we both knew what the question meant.

Without hesitation, she smiled at me with a nod.

'We've always been in this together, right?' she said softly.

It was absolutely true.

* * *

This time I could sense immediately that this life was different to any other I'd been to before. There was promise here; promise like I'd never felt. I knew it would be pivotally decisive. And unlike lives prior, it wasn't the tail end of it I arrived at – that *we* arrived at. It felt like it was just the beginning...

Vicinity of Ein Feshkha, *the West Bank, Jordan 1952*

His name was Maxime Beaulieu. A Frenchman, a priest and a scientist. He'd always been earthy; feeling connected to soil – what had trod atop it, and all that had eventually lain beneath it. From an early age, he'd had a deep interest in archaeology, in dissecting past lives and understanding their interactions, their plight and their successes, and if any of them ever found their "Truth" or made it to their individual version of Heaven.

It had been this deep interest and dedication that had led to Post Graduate studies and qualification in archaeology. Then, on the other hand, that same ceaseless hunt for Truth had also led him to priesthood. And it was through his training for the priesthood that he'd met the notable Roland de Vaux, quickly becoming an avid pupil of the man, who was himself both priest and scientist.

So, being de Vaux's most avid pupil, naturally he'd been keen to follow the man wherever he led.

This was how Maxime Beaulieu ended up embroiled in the West Bank of Jordan with Roland de Vaux and the hardworking people from the American Schools of Oriental Research (ASOR); on the hunt for the now legendary Qumran Caves and the priceless scrolls these caves contained.

Just then, Maxime, together with a few representatives from de Vaux's team, was meeting with the Sheik Daysam Al Uquab, the chief royal of the Bhari tribe, according to Bedouin customs. The Bedouin being nomadic Arabs who historically inhabited the desert regions stretching from the sands of North Africa to the high dunes of the Middle East.

This Sheik, Daysam Al Uquab, had himself learned of the caves and the scrolls through the grapevine. A rival Sheik of another clan/tribe had been one of the lucky few to handle the first scrolls that had been found by the Bedouin shepherd boy who'd made the initial discovery. From recruited spies and investigators, Al Uquab had come to know of this treasure.

Now the scientists had discovered up to six caves, all containing ancient scrolls. And with the discoveries becoming widely publicised around the world, the value of the scrolls had shot up, with every Bedouin with the means and capabilities now scrambling with the scientists for findings. Competition was heavy in the search for more caves and scrolls.

At the moment, Al Uquab had agreed to meet Maxime and the other representatives. There was a new area that had been found. It apparently had big promise for more caves. They were just then trying to negotiate that area, somehow come to agreement between de Vaux's ASOR and Al Uquab's Bedouin.

This was the situation in which Thato and I found ourselves. At a feast in Al Uquab's luxurious desert tent. A feast hosted in honour of Maxime Beaulieu and his people to try and soften them up for a deal.

I found myself a scraggly desert boy hurrying back and forth with platters to serve the Sheik, his entourage and the honoured guests. I could see Thato clearly. Sitting to the right of the Sheik beside the Sheik's most trusted advisor and commander, Zafir Mubarak.

The gold-coloured robe she wore was long, luxuriously flowing and assorted with expensive beaded jewels, covering half her face with only the eyes showing. But they were brilliant eyes, eyes I would recognise anywhere. Not their altered hazel hue but the spirit behind them. Even though now she was Commander Zafir's daughter and only child, she was still my Thato.

The negotiations between the Sheik and Maxime Beaulieu dragged on between courses and a flowing output of Habbaq tea. At every interval with my scuttling back and forth with the other servants as we catered to our Master and his guests, I made sure to catch Thato's gaze. We exchanged looks.

She didn't know how to leave, and I didn't know how to reach her. Finally, just as Maxime launched into a desperate speech about how he and the ASOR team had been the first on the disputed site and how much headway they'd already made, I signalled to Thato. Inclining my head ever so slightly I let her know that I wanted her to meet me outside.

We would have to find somewhere no one would be able to see us. My head surely would roll if I were glimpsed alone in any capacity with a girl of her high station.

She met me at the back of the tent, trailing after me a few moments after I'd left. We were close to the numerous bustling cooking stations it had taken to feed the negotiation party, but we were well hidden behind barrels of food and other living supplies.

Before I could speak, Thato took my arm, drawing me further behind a barrel.

97

'It's him.' She said breathily. 'The soul recognition is so much clearer now. It's my dad. Maxime Beaulieu is my dad.'

I had never met Farhan back home, but when she spoke like that, with such wonder and conviction, I believed her.

'I've had a soul recognition as well T and it's not a happy one like yours, I'm afraid.' I had to burst her bubble with the reality of our situation. 'The Sheik, Al Uquab and his righthand man Zafir – I *know* them. They're the souls of some very bad men I was involved with centuries ago. Arrius and Fabius. The Sheik is Fabius and Zafir is Arrius. They're soul tied. Like you and Farhan. And their only aim in all the many years and lives has always been fast tracking their souls to Paradise and using the being Logos to do it. You remember Logos? I told you about him...'

'Yes,' Thato answered quickly, eyes widened. 'The supreme being with the powers to transport a soul straight to Paradise. How could I forget!'

'Yeah, well, I know those guys. They're wicked and self-serving to the core, and these caves and the scrolls they're so desperate for – it's more than just the sale value of ancient treasure. There *has* to be more to it. Everything they ever did was for Logos and short-cutting to Paradise.'

It was Pompeii all over again. There had to be something in those caves that led directly to Logos.

I lowered my voice, not risking any chance of being overheard. 'Thato, this might be our chance. If these caves have something to do with Logos, we have to get there before Al Uquab and Zafir. Before anybody!'

I didn't need to add that our very futures depended on it, the look in her hazel eyes showed she understood me perfectly.

'Okay. Yes.' She said. 'You're right. Definitely. But maybe we should go to Maxime Beaulieu. Maybe he can help us. Maybe...'

I had to shake my head. 'T, I know he's Farhan to you – your dad. I know the connection you have with him, but this is beyond all that now. For you and me. If we want to be successful in advancing together, I need to know that you're standing by *me* here.'

She drew down her veil and I saw her face fully for the first time. Small, Arabian-tanned and just beautiful.

'Of course, I stand by you SJ – always.'

I let out a breath, more relieved than I'd expected.

'Okay. Right. Great. So, if my calculations are correct, that meeting in there's going downhill pretty fast. Your father right now is Commander Zafir, and he's leading the Bedouin cave excavating operations – if you can somehow get us a place in his retinue; in his team, we can go with him to all the potential sites, and if any caves are found at all we just have to... somehow... make sure we're the first ones in there.'

Thato nodded. She would have replied and was actually opening her mouth to speak but there was sudden commotion towards the front end of the tent, and before too long, a group was heading straight towards us.

Maxime Beaulieu and his men.

I quickly drew Thato closer, gesturing for her to crouch down with me. All we saw were their booted feet as they stomped off, muttering angrily.

Clearly, just like I'd said, the negotiations hadn't gone well.

We were straightening up from our hiding place when a gruff voice could be heard bellowing from inside the tent.

'Mahra? Where is Mahra?' It was Commander Zafir. 'What's happened to that girl? Mahra?'

Thato cast anxious eyes my way. 'He's looking for me.'

With deft fingers, I helped her pull back her veil and straighten the whole headdress. 'Remember, I'm only a serving boy

– I can only do as I'm told. You need to get Zafir to take me on. Meet me by the palm trees over the eastern dunes at dusk.'

Again, Thato nodded.

We were getting ready to hastily part ways when the strangest sensation came over me. I stopped short. I was tinkling all over.

'What's wrong?' Thato looked back at me, worried. Then stopped as well. She felt it too. 'What's happening?'

'I don't know. It's never been like this before. I have this weird feeling... like...'

'Waking up!'

The moment she said it I knew that that was what was happening. Somehow our souls were being drawn away. Somehow, we were waking up.

I tried to fight it. Strained to stop it. There was still so much more we had to do. The caves. The scrolls. Logos. Our only hope was here.

But when it came down to it, there was nothing I could do.

We were leaving.

Chapter Seven

Grandpa Smitty glowered over us in pyjamas and dressing gown, white, scraggly hair flying in all directions, eyes a little blotchy from sleepiness. He'd been shaking us, and now stood back as we got up.

'Right.' He said gruffly. 'You, young man, into PJs, and you young lady coat on and off with you. I had no idea it'd got so late and you were still here. Your uncle's come to fetch you and he's not too well pleased, I'll have you know. I don't think I would be as well – a young girl spending all kinds of late hours, getting up to Lord only knows!'

Thato had done a sharp intake of breath at the mention of her uncle. She hurried for her shoes and coat. Grandpa Smitty happily ushered her out the door without me even getting a word in.

But before long they were both back. Thato booted up and coat zipped up this time. She had a rueful look.

'Go on,' Grandpa Smitty urged. 'Let him know the new parameters.'

Thato let out a breath. 'Uncle Ishaan says I can't come her anymore. He's upset that I've been spending so much time here...'

'That's understating!' Grandpa Smitty cut in. 'Fuming, the man is positively fuming.'

Thato pursed her lips. 'Anyway, he's not happy about me getting home in the early morning hours either, so he says if we're going to see each at all outside of school it has to be at our house.'

I knew what that meant. Ishaan would have serious eyes on us; no doubt be in surveillance of everything we did. I was dreading the prospect of it already. But for Thato I tried to be optimistic.

'At least it's not a full-on ban,' I said. 'We can still... hang out,' I ended lamely for Grandpa's sake, but Thato understood me.

'That's that then,' Grandpa Smitty had clearly had enough of this late-night drama and was eager to return to his bed. 'You've said your piece to him, lassie. Now off with you. I'm for bed! SJ, I can trust you to see your guests out, can I not?'

I wasn't really keen on facing Ishaan, but Grandpa Smitty was already doddering off in his bedroom slippers. Thato gave another rueful smile and led the way back down.

Ishaan's tall, imposing frame shadowed the living room doorway. Tight-lipped and hard-eyed he was more than a little menacing. I refused to be cowered by him though. The man was obviously a bully; merciless and hard-hearted, wanting to strike fear in all those around him. I greeted him levelly, matching him stony gaze for stony gaze.

'I won't dignify your insolence with politeness,' he responded coldly.

'Uncle!' Thato gasped. 'There's no need to be unpleasant to SJ...'

But Ishaan rounded on her even angrier. 'Don't you dare to tell me what there is and isn't a need for. It is *your* insolence I'm most fed up with, in fact. Ungrateful girl as you are! Disobeying me at every turn. Insulting me by not seeking my permission for anything. Doing exactly as you please – even coming home at all ungodly hours!'

Have I not done everything for you, Thato? Everything for our family; even your equally ingrate of a father! But do you appreciate any of that? Does he? Does anyone? Does fate itself ever smile upon me? All my efforts...

After my departed father, I am one of the very few who have truly kept the way; stayed absolutely true to the way of Veda. I came from a long line of the Brahmins! I have dedicated my life to Veda. Yet it's people like your father, Farhan – selfish, self-serving people, who get to perform the Ashrama; who get to fulfil their Moksha. While the likes of me are stuck in endless temple duties and babysitting *brats*.

And as for Farhan – as idiotic my cousin is, he's probably on the verge of Nirvana!' His eyes had turned bloodshot and he nearly foamed at the mouth with rage as he hurled the final part.

And in that moment, realisation dawned. I couldn't believe I hadn't seen it long before then. It was so obvious, so strikingly clear. I exchanged a look with Thato, seeing the same recognition in her eyes. Just as I'd just become aware, she knew Ishaan from a past life.

Her uncle Ishaan was the Sheik Al Uquab. He was also the Neapolitan of old, Fabius. I didn't comprehend how I'd missed it.

'I'm done with this nonsense,' Ishaan continued to bellow. 'If either of you disobey me again, there will be a great penalty to you both. Don't you ever test me again.'

He grabbed Thato by the arm, leading her towards the door. She gave me a plaintive look at she trotted behind a firmly striding Ishaan.

And with that the stakes were raised even higher.

I absolutely need to act, and fast.

~

There was only one being on whom I could call. The past weeks I'd been deplorable to her; had sent her away actually. I now saw it had been foolish to try at this without her guidance, without her support. With Thato firmly under the thumb of one of my bitterest rivals, I needed that guidance and support more than ever.

Back in my room, I sat myself in the centre, entering a deep meditative state. With all the willpower I could muster, I summoned Ezer.

'I need you,' I intoned softly. 'Help me. Please.'

Ezer didn't disappoint. She appeared in shimmering perfection. This time robbed in vibrant powder blue, the material breathily tender and dusted through with millions of tiny crystals that not so much caught the light as outputted a light of their own.

I stood, never happier to see her.

'Ezer!' I breathed. 'Thank you. Thank you so much for coming.'

She smiled. A literally radiant smile; her entire face softly aglow.

'You don't have to thank me, *Ladaka*. I come when I'm needed. And if you only call on me, I will be here, always.'

I was part choked up with gratitude, realising afresh how idiotic I'd been to send her away as I'd done.

'I'm so sorry, Ezer. The way I've acted...'

'I'm here now, *Ladaka*,' she replied softly. 'Let's proceed; time marches on. You've achieved none of the Dharma Shastra so far.'

I nodded with pursed lips. 'No, Ezer. No, I haven't. But that's why I need your help. I've been to 1952; to the Caves of Qumran. I think a Sheik there, and a Bedouin commander are after a specific cave, a specific scroll – something to do with Logos.'

The Keeper of Nirvana wasted no time in affirming this.

'There was a cave – the 12ᵗʰ cave of Qumran. It contained the Scroll of Logos, before it was stolen in a raid by Commander Zafir in the latter season of 1952. You are quite right, *Ladaka.*'

'But I can go back, right. I can get ahead of them and intercept the Scroll myself? And this Scroll – it can lead straight to Nirvana, can't it?

I didn't add that my intention was to use it for Thato and myself both. Though, I think, the Keeper being an eternal being, she already knew that much. As well as already knowing that nothing she could ever say could dissuade me from including Thato. She was my strongest soul-tie; my soulmate; nothing could ever detract from that, and that fact alone meant I would always be all in for her and she would always be all in for me.

'It is correct, *Ladaka*. The Scroll leads to Logos himself and once you meet Him, the only destination is Paradise. He is the direct path. But in terms of going back; back to that specific time, it would be a path from which there is no return.

Ladaka, you have to speed through so many lives already, and going back to one specific life, as you so request, and living that one to its full conclusion, there can be no other life – or lives – after that. This one life, the Qumran Caves 1952, will be your one and only chance.'

My shoulders fell, my whole frame sank.

'If you should not succeed,' Ezer continued, 'there will be no Virtue, and with no Virtue, there is no progressing to Artha or to Kama. Which means no Nirvana. And ultimately, no Paradise. Your soul would be lost, SJ.'

I sank into the nearest seat. I thought through everything she'd just said. It was a blow. Basically, each and everything would be forfeit – curtains; down the drain; played out; game over – if I failed at Qumran.

But if I succeeded... Thato and I, our souls would be freed forever!

Surely that wonderful outcome was worth any risk? And, anyway, if I didn't go through with this Thato was dead for certain by the end of this season. At least if I went back to Qumran, she had a chance. And a single chance was better than no chance at all.

I sat up. Ezer immediately read the resolve in my eyes.

'Alright then,' she said softly. 'Stand up please.'

I stood. I would do this for Thato. I would risk everything.

'Give me your hand,' she indicated my already marked right hand. I readily obeyed and she took it within her own. Then, as she'd done before, seeming so long ago when I'd fallen from Nirvana, she traced over my palm with her finger, creating a blazing trail of light. When she'd finished there was a small new curving mark emblazoned just beneath the Amulet of Atman. An outline vibrant and gold-like.

'You will use this to return to Qumran,' she said. 'You can go back there only twice. One try and a single second chance. Nothing more. Be careful then, *Ladaka*. Be careful and exercise caution.'

She stepped away from me. Her form wafted as she prepared to leave.

'I will be with you along the way, SJ. Always.'

A final shimmer and she was gone, leaving me to stare down at the new tattoo she'd gifted me with.

✳ ✳ ✳

I was at the Farouk-Singh house straight after dinner the next evening. A space steeped in the tradition and culture of the family. In every way; from the vivid colours of the walls to the furnishings and various decorative items, which included religious ornaments set around with reverent precision.

I was ushered by Ishaan through the narrow hallway, past a kitchen to one side, and into the living room. The living room with the same medley of colour that had marked the hallway, but with much more on displace – ornaments, photographs, religious relics.

In the middle of the room, an openly hostile Ishaan faced me coldly.

'I'll let Thato know you're here,' he said in glacial tones. And looking up into those hard, grey eyes, it was an odd emotion that stirred in me. It felt strange for me to be face to face with Fabius again. I vividly remembered stepping over his dead body in Pompeii.

I was relieved that, between us, it was just me who recognised the other from so long ago. Fabius, for all his painstaking efforts, still hadn't transitioned. Also, he didn't have what I had. The ace in the hole, so to speak. The Amulet of Atman. So, there was no way he could know me like I knew him. In spite his hostility, I had that advantage over him.

'You should be aware,' he continued, 'I'll just be in the next room from the library – my prayer room. Anything untoward and that's the end of these so-called tutoring sessions of yours.'

Yes, the tutoring. That's what we eventually decided to go with as our cover story to assuage an already highly displeased and suspicious Ishaan. Thato was helping me prep for GCSE mock exams. We were sticking to that.

Ishaan didn't wait for any response to his open threat. He unceremoniously left me standing there. With nothing else to do except wait for Thato to come down, I paced slowly round the compact room, glancing at different photographs hung up or set on display along windowsills.

One photograph caught my attention. I stopped pacing, my heart skipping a beat. It was a picture of Ishaan, an unclear outdoor backdrop behind him. Standing next to him was a much older man. I didn't know the face but the eyes... the eyes gleamed with a particular look that stirred something inside me. It was a look I would know anywhere. I'd had so much experience with that look. It was the look of the man I'd wrestled to death – his death – some six score years ago. Fabius's twin brother, Arrius.

There was obviously a far-reaching soul-tie here, I thought looking closely at the framed photograph.

Thato came in at that point. She saw me staring at the photograph.

'Oh, yes, the shrine of our family moments,' she said coming up behind me.

I straightened from hunching over the frame. 'Hi.'

'Hi,' she replied. Then faced the wall I'd been looking at so intently. She pointed to one of the multiple pictures. A colour-filled, celebratory-themed one. 'Uncle Ishaan and Aunt Nadra, of course. On their wedding day. Uhm, my dad at a local charity event,' she was pointing at a picture of a tall, lean man – not lean and muscular like her uncle but more of a delicate leanness, like he was fragile somehow. He was bespectacled, with a wide smile on his face. But despite that brilliant smile, a type of sadness seemed to mark his features – especially the eyes. The eyes seemed old, ancient even, filled with lifetimes of trials. This was a soul that had been in circulation for a very long time. Far longer than I, or anyone else I knew or had known.

He was wearing a *kurta*, his arms and the top of his chest visible. The entire length of the arms, the neck, chest, the legs, everywhere, was intricately tattooed; like his body had been made a canvas; basically, a map on which to read his devoutness. Unlike Ishaan's inkwork of prideful display of social status, what marked Farhan seemed to cry out desperation and dedication.

'It was just before he finally left, for good.' Thato said softly, thoughtfully. Next she pointed to a portrait of a fair-skinned raven-haired young woman, with rosy cheeks and large brown eyes. 'And that was Riya. Mama.' Her breath caught a little, her voice cracking.

I let her have a moment. When the emotion passed, I asked, 'And this man?' Pointing to Ishaan and the older man. 'Who's this man?'

'Oh, that's Uncle Ishaan's father. Grandpa Paschim. My dad told me how devastated my uncle was some years back when Grandpa Paschim died... Terrible brain tumour. They were thick as thieves those two.'

'I'll bet they were,' I intoned.

Thato looked at me questioningly.

'T,' I began. 'Your Grandpa Paschim, he was Fabius's twin brother back in Pompeii.'

Thato blinked. 'Really?'

'Oh, yeah. Trust me, I would know the guy anywhere. Him and your uncle; they have a relational soul-tie – like you and your dad.'

'Wow,' Thato shook her head, taking it in. 'All this still totally blows my mind. We should get on, yeah? It's getting late and if we do manage to go back to Qumran we need to really keep track of time. I don't think Uncle Ishaan's full-on sold on this tutoring thing. We need to stick to his rules or he'll just blow up again – even more than the last time, if possible.'

She didn't need to say it twice. I followed her to the library, along the way filling her in on Ezer and how she'd agreed to let me travel back to that December in the West Bank. And it was hard to also relay the fact that we had just one shot at this. But I had done some research earlier on the Qumran Caves and the scrolls – the Dead Sea Scrolls, as they were now called, saying as much to her.

She led the way into the family library. 'Qumran Caves. Dead Sea Scrolls. I remember something like that from one of my classes. History, was it? Or Geo? Didn't they discover another cave in recent times or something like that?'

We were sitting at a study table in the middle of the room now.

I nodded. 'Yeah, exactly. In 2017 the 12th cave was discovered. But get this... it was empty. And there were signs of looting. From what I read, archaeologists believe it was looted in the 50s, round about the same time de Vaux and his team were still working in the area.'

'That banquet!' Thato exclaimed. 'The one the Sheik held for Maxime Beaulieu and his men. They'd been disputing a site. You think the Sheik or Commander Zafir found a cave there first and looted it before de Vaux and his people got to it?'

'I don't think it, T, I know it. And obviously, if your Grandad Paschim was Arrius, he was also Commander Zafir, which means Zafir probably didn't make it past the early 50s – maybe not even past that December of 1952. I can't think of anything except that he's the one who found the Scroll of Logos. If he somehow failed to use it or passed it on for some reason, I don't know. But what's for sure is that we have to go back and make sure it's us that get there first this time. Whoever took the Scroll, we have to beat them to it.'

'I'm ready if you are.' Thato offered me her hand across the table. With Ezer's new marking still throbbing fresh on my palm, I reached for the hand.

The West Bank, Jordan
Dec, 1952

We were back outside the tent of Sheik Daysam Al Uquab, crouched among the barrels of royal household supplies. Commander Zafir was still calling for his daughter, Mahra. I looked to Thato.

'Mahra, you're up.'

She smoothed the folds of her floor-length bright robe. I could sense her smiling behind the veil over her face. She was as geared up as I was for this. We would outsmart the Commander and the Sheik and be the ones to, at the end of it all, hold up the fabled Scroll of Logos. We were together. We were stronger together.

I waited some minutes before following her back into the tent. When I went in there was a flurry of activity going on. Servants were clearing away the remnants of the badly concluded meal. Zafir was being helped into travel clothes by two other servants, Thato standing beside him as he ordered still more servants to go to his tent and begin packing immediately.

The Sheik meanwhile sat on a lofty seat in the centre of the bustle, overlooking everything with a hard stare. From the clench of his jaw and the granite set of his bearded face, I could tell that he was himself as displeased and frustrated as the scientist Maxime Beaulieu who'd just moments before stormed off.

'We'll depart at once, sire,' Zafir was saying now to the fuming Sheik. 'They won't be anywhere near the site before noon tomorrow at best. If we leave now and ride hard till dark, we're guaranteed to make the vicinity by dawn. I've studied the map we procured from the shepherds; we can't fail to find that cave.'

Procured, he'd said. I could have scoffed. Zafir had raided several homesteads the shepherds kept to get that map. Him and his small bank of hooligans he liked to call soldiers had mercilessly beaten the shepherds, leaving a few of them near dead. *Procured* was too civilized a word for the barbarism they'd carried out.

'You get there first, Zafir,' the Sheik growled. 'I had a time of it even getting that map. Do you know the amount of gold I had to toss at paltry fools. The number of people I had to have executed for standing in my way. The distances I travelled. Just for a chance at that which we've heard of for so long.

We're nearly there now. It's practically laid at laps now. We only have to get there first. Those filthy ASOR scientist cannot, *cannot* get there before us.'

Fully robed, complete with turban, Zafir bowed low to his master. 'I vow to you, Highness, I will not let you down.' He straightened and shouted to his servants, 'Come! Not a moment to waste. My horse, is it ready?'

He was already striding towards the flapped exit of the tent. A nervous serving man trotted behind him.

'Sir,' the server tremored, 'there are still the supplies to be packed up. We're just in the process of...'

Zafir growled more viciously than the Sheik'd done a few moments before, violently shoving the man aside. 'Well, to it then. Time is of the essence here!' He strode, half stormed through the tent exit parting.

From my background position, pretending to be busy with brushing up a corner of Al Uquab's luxurious tent, I saw Thato follow the commander out. Instantly, I dropped the broom I'd been mock swaying and picked up platters of discarded food, rushing out after them.

Thato was facing the commander as supplies were brought to him and his men.

'Let me come with you, Father,' I could hear her demand in a voice that didn't waver. 'You know my talents for direction and efficient function. I will be indispensable to you, as I always have been.'

Grabbing hold of the reigns of his Arabian stallion, Zafir couldn't argue with that. It would not be the first time his daughter would have gone on campaign with him. She'd accompanied him on numerous other sufficiently dangerous missions before. And exactly as she'd stated, she'd always been indispensable to him. The Commander had taught her well, right from infancy. And to him, who had no other children, she absolutely had the mettle of ten sons. He readily agreed for her to accompany him again.

'Go. Make ready,' he ordered. 'We leave, now.'

'And my servants,' Thato made a push for me to go along as well. 'I will need a few of them to assist me. Not many, just one or two, perhaps. A boy and...'

But the commander was already shaking his head. 'No one else. We are carrying too many supplies as it is already. More people will only put a strain on what we have. Just you. And if you're not ready when the Sheik gives us a parting blessing, we leave you behind.' His decisive tone brooked no argument, and Thato knew not to press him.

Stepping away from the commander who directly mounted his horse, she glanced towards me, an apologetic expression on her face. Then she was hurrying to ready herself for the journey ahead.

I shrank back, disappointed; not able to even so much as approach her in the midst of so many people.

I would have to find my own way after all.

A lowly servant boy with no resources – not even a donkey to my name. That presented an unanticipated challenge.

~

When it came to it, all I could do was trail their group. Some bread wrapped in ragged cloth and water in a goat's skin container slung over my back in a makeshift rucksack, both swiped from the Sheik's household stores.

Riding on donkey – also stolen from the Sheik's stores – I kept to the fringes, hunched low in the saddle; keeping well behind and within the cover of the many sand dunes the desert readily provided. I was careful not to be spotted.

On the best bred and best kept Arabian stallions, the designated party outstripped me easily, but I followed close on their trail, which was embedded in the late afternoon sand.

I didn't have a fully formulated plan as yet. My main goal at that point was to keep up, possibly observe and eavesdrop when I could get near enough. Maybe speak to Thato at a given chance.

The day light faded fast though. It became harder for me to make out the tracks in the sand, as the distance between me and Zafir's party stretched and the winds of the desert were quick to sweep over any marks, leaving only neat, flawless waves of soil.

I was lucky that they stopped to make camp sooner than expected. I had thought Zafir would be determined to ride through the night. But stop they did. Unwittingly providing me the chance to finally catch up.

I watched them from a distance, as they unloaded and unpacked some their stores. Lighting fires. Setting up for the night.

Shivering in my fully body-wrapping but still not entirely adequate *kaftan*, behind some concealing sand dunes, I was unable to light my own fire to ward off the nighttime desert freeze. In the pitch black, desert plains that would have been like a flashing beckon altering Zafir and co. to my presence.

I had to clench my jaw, cling ever more to the *kaftan* and wait for the camp to fall asleep. There would be a look-out shift among them of course. At least one person up in rotation to watch throughout the night. But evading one pair of eyes was more manageable than a camp-full, I reasoned. So, I waited.

When Zafir finally spread out his own blanket and curled over to sleep, I breathed a sigh of relief. He was the last one down. Besides a look-out at the front of the camp, no one else was awake.

I chose my moment carefully, moving swiftly yet undetectably towards the now dead-quiet camp. I had seen where Thato had lain down for the night. Not wasting any time, I edged my way there. In all my lives I'd never been a ninja, but I certainly moved like one that night.

She started only a little when I got to her, a hand immediately on her mouth, but she wasn't surprised to see me. She'd known I wouldn't have been far behind.

I gestured in the direction of the dunes where I'd left my donkey, tether pinned to the ground, and my meagre supplies bunched up in a hastily dug hole. I wanted her to follow me.

Reading the signs, she understood me, but raised a hand to stop me. There was something she wanted to do first.

From inside the folds of her garments, she brought out a jar. She opened it. A powdery, red substance filled it up to the brim. I recognised the powder; had seen it used many times before as a servant boy in the royal household. It was a herbal remedy, a digestive of sorts to treat stiffened bowls. The Sheik was notorious among servers for his troubled and troublesome bowl movements – or, rather, lack thereof. The powders helped him... purge (as he liked to say) ... easier.

At first, I didn't know where Thato was going with this. But she pointed to the horses. It clicked in my mind then. How would we be able to get ahead of Zafir and his team? If their horses suddenly took ill, they would be routed, forced to a standstill.

The digestive powders would have the horses immobile with sickness for a good few hours. More than enough time for Thato and I to zip ahead – we would obviously need to keep one undrugged for ourselves. The other horses would eventually recover, but not before we were miles ahead. It was fail-safe.

We got straight to it, spiking the horses' drinking water, while making sure that just the one didn't drink. We'd evaded the designated look-out and were moments from successfully saddling up the one untainted stallion.

'Mahra?'

We both jumped.

Zafir himself was in front of us, tall and imposing; catching us right in the act of dusting off sabotage powder from our hands, while saddling up his very own horse.

'What is this?' Anger inflected his voice as he took in the tableau we presented.

'Father...' Thato's voice was breathy nerves as she began.

He didn't wait for her to finish, seeing the incriminating jar in her hands and snatching it from her. 'Malina powder?' Then looking to where we'd just straightened from. 'The horses' drinking trough? You put this in the horses' drinking trough?'

'Father, I can explain...' Thato was grasping.

The Commander was having none of it. He threw the jar down in disgust before grabbing hold of us both. With the raised voices, the whole camp was roused by now.

'You filthy scum!' this was directed at me. 'You put her up to this, didn't you? I've seen the way you look at her. Seen your little closeted meetings when you think no one is looking. What do you possibly hope to gain by doing this? Who are you working for? Is it that snake Beaulieu? Or de Vaux himself? Or perhaps a rival Sheik?' he was violently shaking me now. 'Answer me, you wretch! Answer me now!'

'Father, please!' Thato attempted to supplicate again.

'You, shut up!' Zafir shouted in her face. 'You've disgraced me here today. DISGRACED.' He called for his men, voice like thunder in the stillness of the night. 'Get these two out of my sight! I want them bound and gagged.'

Simultaneously, he threw us both face down into the dirt. Strong hands of muscular soldiers grabbed at us as soon as we hit the dirt. They yanked us to our feet to be bound and gagged as Commander Zafir had ordered.

I fought those hands furiously, and in my peripheral vision, I could see Thato doing the same. They had to call over more men to effectively retrain us, we were flailing so much.

They started with the binding. Interlacing tough twine around our wrists. Still we fought. They were about to bring annoyed clenched fists down on us when Thato managed to bite the hand of one of her captors.

He yelled out as the skin broke and blood trickled.

Taking up the opportunity of his distraction, I caught him between the legs with a well-aimed kick. The man writhed to the ground. Instantly, I also caught another soldier behind me, getting him dead in the face with a back-aimed headbutt. The confusion was exactly enough for Thato and I to scamper away.

'What in the devil is happening over there?' Zafir shouted, furious.

Before he or the rest of his group could reach us, we'd got hold of his spectacular stallion again.

I hopped on, pulling Thato up behind me.

The last thing we heard as we galloped away, exactly as if our lives depended on it – which they probably actually did – was the sound of Zafir's blood-thirsty raging.

They wouldn't be coming after us any time soon. The rest of the horses had already been showing signs of extreme sickness. We'd got away. We would be ahead in the race to the site. And if there was any cave at all to be found there, we would be the first ones in.

Thato clinging to my back, the night air rushing in our faces, the exhilaration we felt was palpable.

I looked back at Thato, catching the fiery gleam in her own eyes. But the moment was lost much too soon. Even as we rode on, I could feel us fading, our souls loosing from the bodies they'd been inhabiting. We were leaving again. We were waking up.

Chapter Eight

She sat across from me back at the library table. She spoke first.

'That was incredible,' she breathed.

I agreed. 'But that just leaves one more shot after this. One more shot at the Scroll that can save our souls.'

'At least we got away from Zafir. We have the lead.'

'For how much longer, though?' I made to get up but stopped. Thato's hand; it was glowing.

She saw my awed gaze, following it down to where it rested, and gasped. The tattoo on her palm was not faint anymore. In fact, it was emboldened and luminous.

'This is bad, isn't it?' her brow furrowed. 'I'm not supposed to have this, am I?'

I scrapped back my chair, going over to crouch beside her instantly. 'Let's not panic just yet. It may not be permanent. It may soon fade away or it could be a blessing for us in some way. I'll ask Ezer. She'll know what it means – what to do.'

Some of the panic waned off Thato's face. She nodded. Then;

'I've been thinking SJ...'

I straightened, perched on the edge of the table and waited for it. She continued, 'You know how my uncle Ishaan is the soul of that Neapolitan Fabius, and Grandpa Paschim possessed Fabius's twin's soul? Doesn't this mean that after Qumran their souls still cycled? They didn't reach Nirvana or Paradise or anything at all. If the Scroll of Logos was found by either of them then somehow, they didn't get the chance to use it.'

I could tell immediately where she was going with this. 'It's possible that the Scroll is still out there somewhere to this day!'

'What if we found it, here, now?' her eyes had the same glow that lit up a fire in mine. 'That would give us another chance at it – in the present.'

I stood, rejuvenated in a split second.

'We could use the Scroll of Logos to fast track our souls straight to Paradise from right here!' I was sailing from high to high now. Thato smiled.

But there was still the matter of actually finding it. We couldn't know for sure what had happened to the Scroll all those years ago. And it could be anywhere. What hope had we of ever finding it – of knowing what had happened at Qumran the day Cave 12 was raided. Anything could have happened. Again, it could be anywhere.

Thato seemed to follow my train of thought exactly because the beaming look on her face faded in time to mine.

'We have to at least try,' she encouraged quietly though.

'Yeah.' I knew she was right. At this point all we had was attempt. Everything to gain, everything to lose.

In the middle of our individual ensuing reveries, a floorboard creaked from just outside the door. Thato and I exchanged looks. In the next fraction of a second, I was up and throwing the door open.

My heart strangled in my throat when I saw Ishaan standing there. He wasn't startled at all by my sudden opening of the door. Didn't even try to disguise the fact that he'd been standing there. And there was a strange look on his face.

My mind raced. Directly behind me, I could imagine Thato's doing the same as well. I knew we were both thinking it: How long had the man been standing there? How much had he heard?

The coldness on his face was inscrutable though as he said; 'You done here? Good. On your way then, young man.'

For a moment I debated confronting him, asking him straight up what he'd heard. But if he hadn't heard much at all then that would, no doubt, only waken his already scale-high suspicions. And, on the other hand, if he'd heard the lot then my confrontation would only force discourse and an escalation of the situation. Besides, I couldn't be sure he understood or believed any of it.

At the close of it, I could only turn back to Thato, quietly say my goodbyes.

'I'll see you at school,' she replied in subdued tones of her own. We were both of us on high alert now, and never was I more reluctant to leave her than at that point. I couldn't help thinking what the consequences would be if Ishaan had heard every word, taken every word to heart.

I remembered his tirade against his self-labelled "lousy fortunes".

I have dedicated my life to Veda, he'd raged. *Yet it's people like... Farhan... who get to fulfil their Moksha.*

Who was I kidding that he wouldn't understand or believe. Even now, the man was still as obsessed with spiritual advancement as he'd been in 79AD.

Getting the Scroll had never been more imperative than it was just them. If not in the previous life in Qumran, then Thato and I had to find a way to it in this life.

We would try everything.

~

I got home to find Grandpa Smitty waiting for me. Only it wasn't really him. Within a moment I recognised Ezer within him. She'd heard my heart's cry, the unsettling worry. About Thato and the implant of the amulet I'd unintentionally given her.

Standing in the centre of our drawing room, wearing the familiar form of my grandfather, she beckoned me closer.

'Do you see now, *Ladaka*?' she said in the gruff tones of Grandpa Smitty, though with her inflection the gruffness was tempered somewhat. 'Why I did not allocate this girl to be involved in your sacred quest?'

I shook my head, incredulous. 'Wasn't that the whole point? To change fate? Terrible destiny?'

'It may not be for the better, though,' Ezer warned. 'Trying to alter fate; her fate. And now you yourself have just one more life – a single attempt – before it's all over... Only the Heaven knows if that will be for the better also.'

We were nearly toe-to-toe now, in a mirror image to what was going on internally between us. As if physically at odds with each other. She was the Keeper of Nirvana. She was also my Helper; a guardian spirit. She led and advised. But it wasn't mandatory for me to blindly follow or to necessarily agree with all she said.

I faced her squarely, standing my ground, precarious and uncertain though I was.

'You've unwittingly given your Thato enormous power,' she went on. 'Not only does she now have the gift of soul-recognition; she also has that ability, which was granted to you specifically, to travel between lives – and because she's not under the sanctions that govern you, her ability is... limitless.

Lives before; lives to come; lives parallel – thanks to you, and your disregard of the rules, Thato can now traverse them all. Every action has a reaction, *Ladaka*. And where this new reaction will take her – or you – it is all indeterminate now.'

Her words settled heavily on me. And although I took to heart everything she said, one thing in particular struck me. About lives – those before, those to come and those parallel. Thato now had the ability to travel through them all at will.

We needed the Scroll of Logos, she and I. We needed to know what happened to it. If Arrius had kept it or not, used it or failed to, and how and why he'd failed.

I only had one life left, and that I needed for the race to Cave 12 at Qumran. But Thato... Thato now, in a sense, had multiple lives at her disposal. Through her, surely, we could go back to when Arrius found the Scroll. See for ourselves what had happened! Possibly even locate the Scroll of Logos right now, in present times.

With expectation, I looked up at Ezer, ready to plead for this fresh plan.

Ezer, though, knew already what I'd been thinking. With the stern face of Grandpa Smitty, she regarded me levelly.

'If you must, you must, *Ladaka*,' she said simply.

My heart was thudding with renewed hope.

It wasn't a no.

And when I met up with Thato later in the day, in between classes, I was exuberant, eager to relate to her my conversation with Ezer.

Patrick, though, coming up behind her out of sixth form Science Class threw something of a ranch in my plans. Derailed me from immediately speaking to Thato by quickly cutting in front of her, in that self-elevating, no-regard-for- "lesser"-beings way that only he could manage.

'Been a bit of a ghost, haven't you, mate,' he got in before Thato could open her mouth to say a word.

Patrick shook his head, a derisive look on his face. 'Flaming drama club. Waste of bloody time, buddy!' He gave me a condescending pat on the back. 'Lemme know when you wise up and we can kill it on the football pitch, yeah?' He chuckled lightly at his own statement he thought pretty funny.

Without acknowledging Thato, who now stood with me, he sauntered off full of self-importance.

Thato shook her head. 'I don't know how you stand that guy. That you're even friends with him... gosh. Yeah, anyway. Leave to the gutter what belongs in the gutter, right? I take it you've come up with some brilliant plan about the Scroll and are now going to lighten my soul with your awesomeness!'

I lifted a shoulder. 'I don't know about brilliance or awesomeness, but there is a way to know what happened to the Scroll. And, another thing, we need to talk about your Amulet.'

She walked with me to my next class as I laid the whole story on her. What Ezer had said about her tattoo and its powers. What I thought we could do to get to the bottom of the Scroll whereabouts. How to do it.

She was looking at me mouth agape by the time I was done. We stopped just outside of my class.

'Wow!' was all she could manage in that moment. In the next, she was geared up and itching to get going. 'So, what time are you coming to my house tonight?'

'That's just it, Thato. With the Amulet you have there're no fixed rules. I mean, soul travel can be anytime, anywhere... anyhow.'

I let that sink in a moment.

And when we came together again at the end of lessons, sitting down together by the fountain in the Remembrance Garden, she was still trying to let it settle; trying to wrap her mind around it.

'So, we don't sleep?' she asked for like the sixth time that day. 'We just... go?'

I nodded. Again. '...Anyhow.'

I could tell she was nervous, and not wanting to let over-thinking or overt-talking add to those nerves, I called a time-out by offering her my left hand, without the Amulet on it. The time for discussion was over. Do or die.

Cautiously, she brought her tattooed hand to the hand I offered. She clasped it.

In a burst we were in Qumran's Cave 12, at the exact moment Arrius found the Scroll of Logos.

* * *

The Scroll of Logos was held high in his right hand. Commander Zafir fought to stand his ground on the only platform in the dingy but spacious cave. A dusty, bedraggled mess, robe in tatters, turban long fallen to the dirt covered floor and dark hair matted by perspiration onto his head, he wielded a sword with frantic yet expertly controlled speed.

They were men fighting him. Men after the Scroll just as he'd been. Men dressed in the sashed robes of his own troop. Traitors.

Thato and I stood back against the walls of Cave 12, the action unfolding rapidly in front of us.

One moment Zafir had the upper hand, cutting down all of his opponents with fluid, well-aimed thrusts that drew blood. The next minute he had a sword plunged directly into his side by one of the mortally wounded men at his feet.

In bursts of thick, dark red, the blood flowed out of his mouth. He gurgled. Once. Twice. And that was it. His eyes rolled back into his skull. He crumpled to the ground, his garments already staining damp the at the piercing.

The Scroll he'd been clutching onto unfurled from laxed fingers, falling into a crevice behind.

The man who'd plunged the knife growled, scampering on trembling scuffed hands towards it. He was groaning and gasping with the effort. Ultimately, the effort proved too much as he too succumbed to his injuries. Just a fraction of a second away from where the Scroll had fallen, he stopped, dead.

127

We were travelling again before we could so much as move, our souls and incorporeal bodies traversing time. Day after day. Night after night. Season after season. Till the bodies of Zafir and his treacherous band became nothing but bones and dust. Till another shepherd stumbled on to the cave, wandered in unwittingly; curiously looked about, and, thanks to the blasts of war that had at a point overcome the region, the crevice where Zafir had dropped the Scroll lay exposed. The shepherd boy saw the Scroll. Hadn't the slightest idea what it was but decided to take it anyway.

Riding as if on the breath of the supernatural, we followed him to the humble home that he shared with an extended family. How his father seized upon the Scroll, sold it to a merchant for close to nothing; the merchant who in turn sold it to a Sultan for more money than the shepherd boy or his father would ever see in their lifetimes combined. And the Sultan who himself, after a number of years, gifted it to an English Lord.

Our souls, our bodies spiralled up and away just then, in what was like a gust of smog and wind.

As the wind settled and the smog cleared, we found ourselves back in the Remembrance Garden, and it was as though not a single minute had passed. We were right back to the very moment we'd left; to the very second in fact.

I faced Thato, excitement mounting. 'I know that Lord. When I was little, he used to play with me and... Patrick. Thato, that Lord was Lord Astley the Ninth. As in...'

'Patrick's grandfather!' Thato finished with a flurry.

I smiled at her. 'I know where the Scroll is.'

Chapter Nine

Thato drove. The vintage minivan she'd scored at a discounted price from a family friend working its hardest as she put foot. We were racing to Brighton Manor; the home Patrick shared with his parents; his ancestral home.

'Patrick's grandfather was always big on artefacts,' I explained to Thato as she navigated the narrow roads of a grey and overcast Carbarney.

'He literally went 'round the globe collecting all kinds of old precious pieces. I mean, the man was kinda obsessed. I remember as a kid, Patrick and I would just be in total wonder at the amount of stuff he had. Hundreds and hundreds of collector's items. And he had them all stored and displayed in the Manor basement – had like a mini-museum going on down there.'

'It must have been pretty impressive,' Thato surmised.

I nodded. 'It was. Just, absolutely spectacular. I can't even remember the Scroll ever being there – ever seeing it or noticing it. There was so much stuff. Anyway, back then I wouldn't have had a clue as to the value; the power it had. Mad.'

'So, all those years ago, he must have bought the Scroll from the Sultan to add to his massive personal collection.' She was pulling up to the Brighton Manor driveway. 'Same as you, neither he nor the Sultan had the slightest idea of what the Scroll actually was, what it was capable of.' She rolled down her window for me to announce ourselves through the intercom.

A moment later, the great gates enclosing the Manor slowly drew apart, opening a way for our car to enter.

Patrick was waiting for us at the front door, fully kitted in his football gear. Clearly, we'd interrupted him just as he was making ready to leave for football practise. He frowned, seemed annoyed as we got out the car.

'Hey,' was his brief greeting as we met him at the top of the short flight of stairs leading to the wide front door. 'So, what is this super urgent favour you need? You sent me like five hundred texts!'

I cut straight to it: 'Patrick, remember when we were kids your grandad had this massive collection of archaeological artefacts?'

'Yeah?' Patrick frowned again, obviously wondering where this was leading.

'I need to have a look at that collection, Patrick. There's this Scroll. I *need* to find that Scroll.'

'Well, you're gonna have a tough time of that, mate,' he was blasé, and it was my turn to frown.

'Why is that?'

'There was a fire in the basement in 2010 – think that was the time you spent the summer up North with your mum's folks. Everything was burned to a crisp by the time they managed to stop the blaze. Nearly took down the Manor – repairs were a nightmare, remember?'

My heart completely sank.

Now, I remembered.

III

Ein Feshkha/Qumran Caves, the Dead Sea, December 25, 1952

We were riding hard on the desert sands, sands that seemed to stretch endlessly into a horizon so distant it made us feel as if we could ride forever and never reach anything; never get to a tangible destination.

The early morning sun was creeping up slowly, already bringing that keen heat that would only become worse as the day wore on; the promise of scorching heat.

The luxury of time we'd enjoyed until that point was fully lapsed. It was firmly a case of last chance before curtains now.

I don't think either Thato or me ever had anything so much in the fore of our minds as we did in that moment, about how utterly important it was that we get to the Scroll Cave first. With the fire at Brighton Manor, if Zafir were to get there before us it would mean the Scroll of Logos would literally be lost forever.

When we fled the Commander that previous night, we'd had little in the way of plans except to get as much distance as possible between us and him. But as the night turned to morning, we'd decided that our best bet would be to align with Maxime Beaulieu.

He'd left a short while before our expedition with Zafir started. He would still be en route to joining Roland de Vaux and the rest of the ASOR team. He had supplies; manpower; everything we would need to make it to Cave 12 ahead of Zafir.

Finally catching up with Beaulieu, just as dawn cracked, lined up perfectly with our purposes. Him and his people were packing up camp just as we came on them; loading up camels, refreshing horses and gearing up for further travel.

I looked back at Thato. 'You have it all ready?' I asked her.

She nodded, knowing exactly what I meant.

To Maxime Beaulieu, Sheik Al Uquab was in a sense the enemy, the chief rival in the race for Qumran. And we were coming from the Sheik. It would take a lot on our part to convince Beaulieu of our intentions; that we weren't just spies sent out by Al Uquab to lead him astray or some other cunning way to derail his mission and advance Al Uquab's.

We needed Beaulieu to trust us.

Thato hadn't liked my idea, didn't feel right or good about deceiving the man who beneath the exterior was still the father she loved very deeply. But she understood that at this point we had very few options. Lying to Beaulieu would have to be part of the deal.

And Beaulieu himself was the first one to spot us as we approached his camp. He immediately grabbed his rifle and stood on alert; the others with him quickly following suit.

'Ask them what they're doing here,' he threw at a man behind him, presumably their translator because he was also Arab.

'We are not here to cause any trouble,' I said, raising my hands. Thato did the same. 'We just want to talk – make a deal.'

I could tell that my speaking in perfect English threw Beaulieu a bit. He was a Frenchman, but he also spoke perfect English. It just never occurred to him that an Arab servant boy would be able to do the same.

Their weapons were lowered. He was curious and interested now.

'Off your horse then,' he ordered curtly. 'And slowly, please.'

We did as we'd been bid, slowly dismounting while a dozen pair of suspicious eyes were trained unflinchingly on us.

'Out with it then,' Beaulieu was impatient, open to be convinced.

'We have this.' Thato came up from behind me, holding up the piece of parchment she'd managed to slip from Zafir's travel bag. 'It's my father's map. My father, Commander Zafir Mubarak. It points to the location of the cave you were negotiating for with the Sheik.'

Beaulieu made a stunned move forward, 'How did you...?'

Thato snatched the parchment out of sight again, holding it firmly behind her back.

'First, you give us your word that you will help us,' I said. 'Your word as a man of the cloth and a respected scientist. You give us that and the map is yours.'

Beaulieu let out a breath of exasperation, folding slim arms across him chest, the cross he wore on a chain around his neck dangling just above the folded arms.

'Fine. Alright then. What is it you need my help with?'

We want safe passage to the Hinterlands,' Thato said, beginning an outline of the story we'd come up with in the earliest hours. 'Not only did I take my father's map, I took a lot of gold as well. Hasib and I wan to marry. Because he is a servant and I am noble – close to royalty – it is not allowed in our tribe for us to do this. So, we're running away to the Hinterlands to marry and start a new life.'

I stepped up again. 'We will ride with you to this cave, depicted on the map. But thereafter, you must give us your word that you will help us evade Commander Zafir and make it to the Hinterlands.'

Beaulieu paused for a moment. He was thinking. With ice-blue eyes moving between Thato and me, I could feel him weighing us up; weighing up this story we'd spun him.

Did he believe us? Was he sold on the idea of us being runaway lovers and not spies?

With the way he was looking at us, still debating with himself, still so suspicious, he didn't seem convinced. But I think, ultimately, the lure of finding the disputed cave won out. As many caves as they could discover, that was what Roland de Vaux had said was their aim. And he was dedicated to de Vaux; dedicated to their work together.

'Agreed,' he said at last. 'I give you my word as a student of the priesthood, and as a dedicated scientist. I will help you to the Hinterlands... in exchange for that map.' He spread out his arms in a grand gesture. 'I know it is not your way, but... Mercy Christmas to you both.' He smiled widely, leathered skin crinkling around his face. 'And welcome to our expedition.'

Cave 12

Back to crossing the desert sands, it was tougher than before. Hours stretched, end to end, brutal. The blazing heat; discomfiture; the difficult terrain of the Qumran area. It all combined to make for far beneath pleasurable travel.

At last, Beaulieu called for stop; a much-needed refresher. We were all bone weary with exhaustion and heat. We set up a few tents to shelter from the scorching rays beating down on us.

Beaulieu invited us into his tent. Though I can't say it was purely graciousness. More to keep a watchful eye on us, I gathered. Thato on the other hand was sold on his graciousness – sold on everything about the man, actually.

To her, he was the bright shining beckon he'd always been. She admired his brilliance as a science scholar and as a student of the Holy Order. I caught her smiles when she looked at him, and didn't need to be told that he reminded her so much of her father back home. Different exterior, but exactly the same man in spirit.

But soon after sitting down in his tent some of that sparkle dimmed for Thato. We were ravenously biting on some travel biscuits when out of nowhere Beaulieu said,

'I could marry you myself, you know. A Christian ceremony. Right here.'

Caught off guard, Thato and I's expressions were simultaneously wide-eyed shock.

Beaulieu slapped a hand to his thigh, triumphantly. 'Aha! I knew it! Judging from your petrified expressions, marriage was never something you were thinking of! There is no planned elopement, is there? The whole story is a farce – a ruse to ride with my party. Now start talking. What' really going on here? Where, *in truth*, are you actually leading us? The Sheik put you up to this, didn't he? Or Zafir? You were supposed infiltrate us? Lead us on a wild goose chase while gathering information for your own uses!'

Thato and I were even more wide-eyed.

'Don't even try to lie to me!' Beaulieu snapped. 'I'm on to you. Now, one of you – talk.'

Thato looked at me. 'I think we should tell him everything.'

'What? No –' I began to protest, but Beaulieu wasn't having it.

'Tell me everything or we pack up and leave you two right here in the middle of nowhere.'

'He's my soul-tie,' Thato lowered her voice to say to me, almost in a whisper. 'My father. I can make him understand.'

In the face of Beaulieu's hardened features and Thato's determination, I had to relent. When she asked to give her and Beaulieu a moment, I got up and, however reluctantly, I left them alone together.

I paced anxiously back and forth near the tent entry way for what seemed the longest time, but in reality couldn't have been more than a half hour.

When Thato finally came out, I almost jumped. Beaulieu was right behind her. I had to blink when I looked at him.

Were my eyes playing tricks or did the man look like he'd been crying?

And even more surprising was his softened tone when he spoke to me.

'I'll see to it that we're ready to get moving again in a short while. We'll do all we can to locate that cave.' With a hand squeeze to my shoulder, he went on to his colleagues.

In askance, I turned to Thato. 'What did you say to him?'

She smiled a little. There were tears in her own eyes as there'd been in Beaulieu's. 'Not really anything I said. More what I showed.'

She told me how she'd used her own amulet to take Beaulieu back; back through their history together. Snippets of who he'd been, who she'd been and what they always were together. It was a momentous thing for them both.

After than she'd explained everything to Beaulieu. About me, about Beaulieu himself; about her and the deaths. And, finally about the Scroll in Cave 12; the Scroll of Logos and how it now was our one and only hope.

He'd been mesmerised, but above all he'd believed her. He was totally for us now.

Thato and I hugged, relieved and hopeful again. We were still in it. It wasn't curtains yet.

'You guys want to get over here!' Beaulieu was yelling from the middle of a group of his people. 'Guess what? Someone's got Christmas cake!'

And so, there we were, huddled up in the heart of the desert, eating Christmas cake and singing carols.

In the middle of the unexpected festivity, Maxime Beaulieu turned to me.

'I understand SJ, your struggle. I can't really say about any other life, but in this life, I have certainly battled internally – spiritually, you know. It's been this hunger, this total drive from an early age that's almost consumed me. Now, knowing your story and seeing some of my own history as well, I find I'm even more... desperate now for that... spiritual satisfaction... that *something...*'

'Moksha.' Thato who'd been close by finished for him. 'Always it's been your passion and dedication. And in the future – in my and SJ's present life – it's finally happening for you, Papa. You've reached the highest level there. And just like it is for us –' Here she linked her hand with mine, smiling hopefully. '– It will be for you too. All of us are a step away from Nirvana; from Paradise.'

'Hey, can anyone else see what I'm seeing here?' It was one of Beaulieu's men, cutting into the singing and chatter. An American from the ASOR team.

We all craned our necks towards where he was looking.

In the horizon, shimmering in the desert like some type of mirage was what seemed to be the opening of a cave.

My heart pounded.

Cave 12?

'*Mon bon Dieu,*' Maxime Beaulieu exclaimed. 'Well, let us not stand around staring. Let us get down there!'

Immediate, thrilled commotion ensued as everybody bustled to get their things together.

The bullets came as a shock.

Suddenly, the air around us was whizzing with gun fire. Behind us: Zafir.

The ever-resourceful military commander had caught up to us, fresh horses no doubt courtesy of the Sheik now bearing him and his men as they vengefully attacked us. His own daughter be damned.

Each of us scrambled for whatever cover we could find. Which wasn't much, considering where we were – bam smack in the plains of the Dead Sea.

Thato, Beaulieu and I, having been beside each other when the attack happened, found ourselves huddled, still together, behind one of the compact but solid expedition carts.

I was breathless and stunned, assumed my companions behind the cart were too. But when I looked over at Thato and Beaulieu, I saw that it was far worse for the priest-scientist.

A large red stain was growing to drench his abdomen. He'd been hit.

At that point Thato followed my eyes. When she saw Beaulieu injured, the extent of it, she let out a cry.

'No! No!' she grabbed onto him, pressing her hand against the leaking wound.

Beaulieu winced. He groaned. 'I – I don't think I'm going to make it.'

Thato shook her head forcefully. 'No. No. You won't die. I won't let that happen!' She turned frantic to me. 'He can't die. Not now. He was supposed to live out more years in this life. Supposed to gain more soul awareness to progress in the next life. If he dies now...'

He's lost.

I didn't say it. Thato didn't say it. But we both thought it.

We'd done this. Without our interference, Zafir wouldn't have come guns blazing to attack Beaulieu's team. Now Beaulieu was fatally wounded. Dying. And he would regress, not progress in spirit if he died now. No Farhan. No adoption. Thato too would be lost. Without the adoption by Farhan and Riya, heaven only knew where she'd end up.

'What do we do?' Her eyes were panicked, gazing up at me.

'We have to make a run for the cave,' I said the only thing we could do. 'There's nothing else. We make it to Cave 12; we all use the Scroll of Logos to progress.'

'All three of us? Will that work?'

'It has to. Grab a hold of his arm. Help me get him up.'

Beaulieu was slipping in and out of consciousness now. We hoisted him up as best as we could. Evading the fire, we started running. Though not so much running as tottering, dragging a staggering Beaulieu between us. Inching closer to Cave 12, it seemed so near yet so far with Zafir and his goons, now out of bullets, and giving chase on horseback.

Pressured and desperate, we picked up pace. In a minute, the cave opening was in front of us. An eroded, partially buried opening we each had to scramble, singularly into – Beaulieu we managed, between us, to pull in; just about getting past the threshold.

Inside it was spacious and resounding; the exterior belying just how vast the interior was.

'The Scroll!' Thato breathed. 'It's right over there!'

I looked up, and sure enough, laid bare in one of the many crevices lining the walls of the musty cave was a large, rolled up parchment.

Beaulieu's ragged, laboured breathing resounding in the hollow space, I made my move towards the Scroll. Relief coursed through me, excitement even. It was happening. It was actually, finally, happening.

At the crevice I reached for the parchment. The weight of it – oddly light, like it wasn't the greatest piece of human hope. The texture of it – the leathery, ridged, but supple quality. Just the general feel of it, was like touching Paradise itself.

I turned it over. And froze.

'SJ, quick, you need to bring it over here – *now*.' Thato cradled Beaulieu's sweat-matted head in her hands, crouched over him.

I complied, closing the small distance between us. But it was with heavy steps.

Thato took one look at me and knew something was wrong.

'What? What is it? He's dying SJ; we need to act now!'

'There's an insignia on the Scroll,' I said softly, showing it to her. It was scrawled gold in Aramaic.

'One body. One soul.' Thato read. 'One eternal gifting.'

'It's only for one person,' I said softly. 'Only one of us can use the Scroll.'

The commotion outside increased. Zafir could be heard raging. They were no more than a few feet away from the cave.

'It has to be Maxime,' I made the spot decision. I would be handing over the paradise ticket that was always supposed to have been mine. 'We caused this. We can't let his soul be forfeit. We can't let you be forfcit.'

Tears came to Thato's eyes. I knew the emotion was not so much for herself as for the two people she loved most. Me and her father. Through decades she'd been strongly tied to both of us. We were both the love of her lives. Understandably, she started to cry.

'You're mine, you worthless scum!' Zafir hollered at the entrance, already shuffling in.

It was now or never.

I carefully placed the Scroll in Beaulieu's hands.

'Maxime. Maxime. You have to open this.' I spoke to him in French, hoping to reach him better with his mother tongue. 'Do you understand? You have to open this Scroll. Maxime!'

The man's eyes opened a sliver. He seemed to have heard me, because with trembling fingers he slowly broke the seal and opened the Scroll.

A flood of bright, white light filled the dark space, making it dazzle. We all shielded our eyes, blinded by the piercing radiance.

When finally I could open my eyes again, everyone was gone; the cave itself was gone.

* * *

I stood alone in an empty void that stretched endless in front of me. Nothing but soft light around me.

Then she was there.

Shimmering in a kaleidoscope of every colour I had ever known, she came to me. Just draped in nothing but revolving colour. Hair the fluid cotton flow of pure white that was trademark to her. The translucent skin. The eyes burning bright orange like two overheated furnaces.

'Ezer,' I breathed, never more glad to see anyone as I was to see her in that moment.

'Congratulations,' she smiled, and it was like a sun rise. 'You've completed the Shastra of Virtue. Your sacrifice for Maxime's greater good was most Virtuous.'

My whole frame weakened. Stunned. Enthralled. Relieved beyond all words. I couldn't believe it.

'I thought it was all over,' my voice broke with emotion. 'When I handed that Scroll over to Beaulieu, I thought it was the end for me.'

'I know you did, *Ladaka*.' Ezer's twin flames glowed, ever more fiery. 'But it's not the end. Now that you've completed the Virtue Shastra, you can move on to completing the other two. It's not over yet.

Artha. Kama. The two Dharma Shastra you still need to achieve. Though for now you've made it past the first level, and you should be in gratitude for that.'

In gratitude? I was so faint with gratitude, I didn't even have the words!

'And because of the stunning display of sacrifice you made at Qumran; you have an extension on your time. More seasons have been added for you to complete the rest of the Dharma Shastra.'

A tear escaped my eye then.

Ezer gently took my hand. 'Keep faith SJ. Keep faith.'

She squeezed my hand and I felt myself fading. My soul was on the move again. Lighter, less burdened, it felt refreshed, and I was energised. I was ready to take on anything.

Chapter Ten

The Andhra village sits deep in the dense forests of the lowlands of Punsari, India. Grandpa Smitty charted a private plane to get us to Mumbai. From Mumbai we'd taken the four-hour train ride to Punsari; then a bus to the small village of Andhra.

A murky river ran through the village, dividing the already tiny land into two even tinier subdivisions. We stood at the river now; by the water's edge. Grandpa Smitty, Thato and I, flanked by the village locals.

When word reached the UK that Farhan had died, it hadn't come as that much of a shock to either Thato or me. In fact, having been through what we'd been through, and knowing what we did, the news came with both grief and joy – mostly joy though. We knew what no one else did.

At present, four holy men who'd lived and followed devotion with Farhan during his time in Andhra, came forward. They had bright, powdery drawings on their bodies; chests bare and loose fitting, white sarongs tied to their waists.

Farhan's body lay on the ground beside, covered with multiple cloths of all colours. With the rest of the small crowd –

children, men and women of the village – we stood watching, reverently as they lifted his remains up.

They laid the cloth-laden body onto a stack of sturdy pieces of interjoined wood that were piled on a narrow dingy.

Tears shining in her eyes, but a small smile on her lips, Thato drew a final vivid orange veil across the length of the body.

She stepped back. In sync, the crowd also stepped back. And the holy men lit a flame, placing it onto the pile of bright cloth, spices and incense that had been Farhan Singh.

The flames caught and blazed. One of the holy men nudged the dingy with a hand, setting it adrift on the water.

The fire now raged, consuming. Dark smoke billowed up into the darkening twilight sky.

I put an arm across Thato's shoulders. She leaned into me.

After so very long, Farhan had found his Nirvana. As for me, I would never stop trying. I would keep the faith. I would be free.

Epilogue

On Carbarney Castle's Oates Theatre stage, the curtain closed on us as we took our bows. The college Drama Club's rendition of Tom Stoppard's Arcadia was a resounding success. The applause rang out long after the curtain fell.

Thato and I, with the rest of the cast, bounded backstage. There was cheering, embracing and kisses. The atmosphere was electric.

In the heart of it, she turned to me.

'So, are we travelling tonight?'

I caught the glint in her eyes; could feel the same glint rising to my own eyes. A sly, half-smile tugged at the corner of my mouth. I took her hand,

'Always.'

Neither of us was aware of Ishaan, merged with clamouring teens, watching us intently from a corner of the room.

Printed in Poland
by Amazon Fulfillment
Poland Sp. z o.o., Wrocław